Rule No.1:

Rule No.1: Avoid Trouble

Mel Symonds

Cover illustrated by Mariya Ali Ameen

Matador
9 Priory Business Park,
Wistow Road, Kibworth Beauchamp,
Leicestershire. LE8 0RX
Tel: 0116 279 2299
Email: books@troubador.co.uk
Web: www.troubador.co.uk/matador
Twitter: @matadorbooks

ISBN 978 1800463 028

British Library Cataloguing in Publication Data.
A catalogue record for this book is available from the British Library.

Printed and bound in Great Britain by 4edge Limited
Typeset in 13pt Minion Pro by Troubador Publishing Ltd, Leicester, UK

Matador is an imprint of Troubador Publishing Ltd

For Vera and Edith,
who know never to get into trouble...

Chapter One

Trouble

I can sense there is about to be trouble. It's kind of like the way Spider-man can sense danger from five miles away. He jumps into action, swings from one building to the next and then when he gets there, he darts out of the way of a flying car at lightning speed.

It's no way near as cool as that, though.

Instead I freeze on the spot while my stomach jumps high up in the air and flips over three times. At the same time, the word TROUBLE is shouted in my ears in a really high, screechy way. So, not really as awesome as Spider-man's sense and I can't really say I got bitten by a spider either. Oh, and it is also not five miles away. It's much closer than that.

It isn't Reggie, who's sitting next to me on our favourite red bench in the school playground. Normally he's moaning about it being cold but today he is happy and chatty because athletics club is on this lunchtime in the school hall. No, I sense there is about to be trouble, because as I'm sitting on my favourite red bench with a football rolling past me and Oscar and Emily running after it, and I'm watching Year 3 have their turn on the climbing frame – I can see Bella. Bella is the cause of my Spider-man-like trouble sense. I can see her marching towards Reggie and me from the school doors. Her brown curly hair is jumping up and down behind her and her face is holding on to an explosion of news. This is when I know deep down, in the pit of my stomach, for absolute certain, that there is about to be a whole heap of trouble.

"Clara, Reggie! You will never guess what I heard!" she shouts at us as she marches over, the last part ending in an attempt at a whisper, as she gets closer to where we are sitting. Standing in front of us, she looks around at the rest of the playground before turning back and throwing her hands in the air.

"Don't tell me athletics club is cancelled!" Reggie jumps in.

"What?! No, it's Tammy and Charlotte."

"Oh no," I say to myself, sliding further down the bench and into my coat, my hands rising up into my sleeves and forming fists inside it. Perhaps if I close my eyes too, she will change the subject and talk about something else, or maybe the bell will miraculously ring, signalling the end of break-time.

"...They are going to try and ruin Mrs Elliot's lesson this afternoon," Bella continues.

"No!" Reggie shouts, sitting up straight and shuffling his body to the edge of the bench so that he's much closer to Bella.

Mrs Elliot is a science teacher. She comes in every two weeks to teach us extra science. When it's not her, it is Ms Cinnamon, who teaches us art. Mr Graveshead, our usual teacher, sits in the corner of the room writing or shaking his head and muttering angrily while he marks our work. His shiny black hair looks like it's sweating and I watch, waiting for it to form into a drip, which will no doubt run down his crinkled forehead. Or (and this really tends to be most of the time) he is not there at all and is mysteriously doing something else in another room of our school.

Reggie and Bella love our extra science lessons with Mrs Elliot. I don't get it. I mean, I get why they like her coming in – Mrs Elliot is brilliant, she really is. She has short brown hair, round brown glasses, she always wears floaty flowery dresses and she shows us stuff. She doesn't just stand there reading or pointing at a screen; she always has something in front of her. Like she once had this mirror, a clear pyramid and a white light. We gathered around with the lights off and watched as she bent the light and then created a rainbow. She once showed us the giant veins on a plant leaf up really close with magnified glasses. Then there was the time we looked under a microscope at all the tiny creatures we found in the pond on our school trip. They looked huge and scary and kind of like man-eating monsters. It was awesome.

I also get why they love the amazing parts too, like when she makes something go all gooey and slimy, or it might completely change colour or fly immediately up in the air and start fizzing and foaming. It's just she'll then say a really, really long word, or lots of small words together really quickly and I wasn't listening. Bella will nod and Reggie will nod and I don't want to feel left out so I nod a few times too. It's easier to stay quiet than to put my hand up and say I don't get it. What if everyone else in the whole class gets it and I'm the only one who doesn't? The rest of the class will laugh. Definitely laugh. Or worse, someone might even roll their eyes and tut really loudly. Then what if I still don't get it even on the second time of Mrs Elliot explaining it to me? That would be so completely and utterly embarrassing!

So, when Bella marches up to us and says that Tammy and Charlotte are going to try and ruin our extra science lesson this afternoon with Mrs Elliot, all I can think of is, *That's a shame*.

"They said something about wanting to stop 'Crazy-Elliot', and something about her black bag," Bella continues.

"What – why?" Reggie questions with a definite panic in his voice.

"Because they are both mean and horrid."

"But, when?" he asks again.

"I heard them by the coats; they said they didn't want to sit through her stupid lesson and that she must have something in her bag that can shake the class up, and if she doesn't, then Tammy said she knew how to shake the class up and then they saw me and they stopped talking."

Reggie ponders this for a moment – he watches Year 3 swinging around on the climbing frame, and then he looks up at the big row of tall trees at the other end of the playground, past the game of football that has stopped while someone goes and gets the ball again, and then he looks back at Bella. "Shake the class up?"

"I know," Bella replies, a worried look all over her screwed-up face.

When Mrs Elliot teaches us chemistry, she brings in a big black bag. She carries it very carefully from the table in the corner of our classroom and gently places it onto the table at the front of the class. It has two big leather handles and a big shiny clasp at the top in the shape of two giant Maltesers. She twists and turns these giant Maltesers before the bag opens wide.

Lots of wondrous glass tubes and science-y looking things have been lifted out of that bag. Once, we all had to put special goggles on as a bright light appeared – I didn't catch the name as I was too busy watching the angry light, which looked like lots of snake tongues reaching out at the space all around it – plus there was a kind of hissing sound filling my ears. It went as quickly as it appeared, and then we were all allowed to take our goggles off.

I think about those snake tongues as I look at Bella's screwed-up face and I must admit the words '*shake the class up*' do form a heavy sick feeling in my throat. But I do really like to avoid trouble. I do really like a peaceful life with no-one shouting at me. I am sure they won't get away with whatever evil plan they have and that someone will stop them.

"We have to stop them," Bella says as if she has just read my mind.

I mumble into my coat, "Why does it have to be us, though?" Not that either of them notices or are listening to me at all.

Slamming her fist down onto her other hand before putting her fists onto her hips, Bella is all fired up and ready to continue her speech. "I look forward to our science lessons with Mrs Elliot," she says. "And this week it's chemistry, my absolute favourite, and I'm not going to let them ruin it, or shake it up, or worse – get Mrs Elliot fired and we never see her again! We must stop them!"

"Yes!" chimes in Reggie, his fist now slamming down onto his other hand too. It seems to be the thing you do when you're all fired up and ready to go. I roll my eyes, not that either of them notices at all.

"We stop them before they can put their evil plan into action!" continues Bella.

"Yes!" shouts Reggie.

"Before they can ruin the one lesson I look forward to!"

"Yes!"

"And we stop them this lunchtime!"

"Ah, wait, I can't do lunchtime – I have athletics club."

"That's OK, because Clara and I will do it!"

"What?" I say loudly, my head popping out of my coat.

"Mrs Elliot drops her bag off to the classroom

just before lunch, so we are going to have to skip break and go straight to the classroom to guard it."

"We will? But I love break."

"And Reggie can join us after athletics club."

"Yes!" he replies enthusiastically. Clearly his confidence in the plan has returned.

"I don't like this at all," I mumble, my fisted hands now up further in my coat and into my jumper sleeves, my head sinking back down into my coat again and my eyes firmly shut. My trouble Spider-man-like sense is going crazy. This is all sounding like a whole heap of potential and disastrous trouble. Trouble! My highly cherished Rule Number One: Avoid Trouble!

Chapter Two

When a Bad Plan Goes Immediately Wrong

Green Grove School's Year 5 classroom – my classroom – is at the top of this massive flight of stairs, around to the right and next to the Year 4 class. I miss being in Year 4 and I miss my favourite teacher, Miss Tully, who is always nice and always speaks quietly. Mr Graveshead mostly shouts.

Running down the corridor like two fire-fighters ready to enter a burning building, Bella and I don't even stop before we burst through the door and into the Year 5 classroom. We run in the room at full speed ready to catch Tammy and Charlotte in the act of ruining our science lesson. This is our plan, using the element of surprise to our advantage.

Through the door, and immediately we run round to the right and straight for the window in the corner of the room and the table under it. This is where Mrs Elliot always leaves her big black bag.

"Ah ha!" Bella shouts unexpectedly as we turn the corner.

There is no-one there. No Tammy and no Charlotte. It's just a bag, sitting on the table next to a cage. Mrs Elliot's abandoned and unsuspecting big black bag with its two-Malteser-like clasp and Harry-the-Hamster's cage, on a table all completely and utterly alone.

"Oh! Strange…" I say, while looking at Bella.

As if we both think the exact same thing at exactly the same time, we jump together in a half-circle. I bring my hands up in a karate chop-like action that I saw someone do once on TV.

"Got ya!" Bella shouts as we jump, our eyes scanning all the tables and chairs and every corner of the room. Still with my hands up ready,

I duck down and have a quick check under the tables too.

"No-one," I say to Bella, shaking my head. "The room is empty."

Bella and I are standing in a quiet and empty room full of empty chairs. Three of the chairs have been tucked under the table in front of them but the rest look as though a stampede of angry elephants just ran straight through the classroom at full speed, knocking every single chair as they went.

Feeling rather deflated, I sit down on one of the brown plastic chairs next to the table that has Mrs Elliot's bag and Harry-the-Hamster's cage on it. I notice that Harry-the-Hamster is also nowhere to be seen, which I'm guessing means he is asleep, as usual, under his pile of paper shavings and cotton wool. I really thought we were going to surprise Tammy and Charlotte and bust their evil plan to pieces. Although, in all honesty, it's not something I've been looking forward to doing all morning, and I hadn't really thought about what I was going to say to them. I was really just planning on following Bella's lead and nodding in all the right places.

Wide-eyed and still standing, Bella looks down at me and then puts her finger over her mouth in an exaggerated 'shush' move. I wasn't going to say anything.

"Clara, you stay here," she whispers. "I'm going to check out the coat hooks."

She nudges her head towards the blue coat hooks, and then, in a way that I have only ever seen done in a pantomime at Christmas, she tip-toes across the room, bringing her knees up really high as she walks. I watch her, wondering if she will do this weird walk the whole way across the room, which she does, and then I give a little sigh for only Harry-the-Hamster to hear (if he wasn't asleep… and a hamster).

As you enter each classroom in our school, there is a place to the left where you put your coat, bag, PE kit, boots and any other things you have with you that day. Our coat area is blue, and Year 4 is yellow. I like yellow. Plus, in Year 4 the yellow coat hooks were somehow always tidy, while in Year 5 the area is always a complete and utter mess – random bits of PE kit all over the place, a pile of school jumpers, and usually a sock or a shoe. It's a mess and a perfect place to hide and wait.

While Bella does whatever it is that she's doing, I do exactly as I am told and stay on my chair. I have never eaten my lunch so quickly in my life, and with a stern look from Bella, I said no to the pudding of jam roly-poly, which gained me very suspicious and quizzical looks from the lunch staff. So, even though I am absolutely stuffed from eating my spaghetti bolognaise so quickly, the part of my brain that looks after my stomach is wondering where the jam roly-poly is, and this is making me feel completely glum.

"They are not hiding by the coat hooks and I can't see them in the corridor," Bella shouts as she walks back to where I'm sitting, a big smile on her face, her hands on her hips and a perfectly normal walk. "We beat them here! I guess now we just sit and wait for them to arrive."

"Unless they have already been and gone," I say before my brain realises the sequence of words that have just come out of my mouth. I think it was preoccupied with the missing jam roly-poly to filter my thoughts before they came jumping out. I instantly want to grab them all and shove them back into my mouth.

Too late now – Bella has stopped smiling.

"Oh no! Clara, you're right! They could have stayed behind when we all went down for lunch, jumped out of the queue and hid under all the rubbish by the coat hooks. Then, all they needed to do was to wait for Mrs Elliot to leave her bag here and then… umm… then, messed around with the contents and went down to lunch."

I had to admit, that plan did sound a lot better than our plan, and especially as it would have meant not rushing lunch, not missing pudding and not missing break-time to sit in a classroom next to a bag.

"But how would we know?" she questions, looking at the motionless big black bag with its shiny two-Malteser-like clasp on top.

"I guess we just sit here and wait until Mrs Elliot arrives, and then we tell her what you heard?" I reply, hoping that this will be our new plan.

Bella nods very, very slowly, her eyes not budging from their fixed stare on Mrs Elliot's bag, and I wonder if she is actually listening to me. "Yeah, sure… oorrrrrr…"

I don't like the sound of this very long '*or*'.

"...we could open the bag and just see if anything looks wrong, like maybe something could have been added, or moved, or if anything looks like it is missing?"

"I don't think we should touch her bag," I say cautiously, my brain now forgetting about the missing jam roly-poly from my stomach and concentrating on my Spider-man-like sense shouting TROUBLE in my ears. It is going crazy. So much so that there is a large brass bell with a wooden handle that sits in the corner of my head and it has engraved on it: '*Rule Number One: Avoid Trouble. Use in the case of an extreme emergency*', and this is now firmly ringing too.

"Come on, Clara," she says with a big smile. "What is the worst that can happen? I'm only going to have a little check. I won't touch anything."

The really funny thing about saying, '*What is the worst that can happen?*' but then not waiting at all for the answer, is that probably you have already thought there isn't one. Well, my answer to Bella's question, '*What is the worst that can happen?*', would have been a whole page of pre-thought-out problems and scenarios, with some added on to the end from some thoughts that would have just occurred to me.

Except she doesn't give me the chance to answer.

The un-funny thing about her asking such a question, is that even with my pre-thought-out list of answers to that question, plus the answers that would have just occurred to me, I still would not have come up with the real answer to the real question: '*What is the worst thing that can happen to you if you decide to open the strange-looking bag of your overly (but clearly not unjustifiably) paranoid teacher who specialises in chemistry?*'

Yes, the *real* answer to the *real* question would never ever have occurred to me.

"Bella, I really don't think you should open the bag..."

Except Bella's eyes are already alight with the temptation – the black pupils at the very centre of her brown eyes are getting bigger and bigger. It is a wild stare that I have only ever seen her do when Zoe brought in some cherry-flavoured sweets to school and Bella said they were her absolute all-time utter favourite. Bella has always been fascinated with Mrs Elliot's big black bag and has wanted to look inside it ever since she first saw it. It must be that same pure sweet cherry-flavoured goodness.

She doesn't even stop to pause, or look back at me, or even question what she's doing. No. Nothing. A giant leap to the bag and she grabs the shiny Malteser-like clasp. With a huge wet smile forming on her wild face, she quickly twists the clasp and opens the bag.

"NO!" I shout as I jump up from my seat, the words ending in a mere whisper as the sound of the letters are sucked out of existence by a huge bellow of grey smoke that shoots up from the bag. The smoke hits the ceiling above us, disperses out at the sides and swiftly drops to the floor. As quickly as it has appeared, it wraps around our feet and starts to circle around our ankles, rising up to our knees, our waist and our shoulders. I cough as the smoke rises above my head and covers my eyes. The dense smoke makes it impossible to move. I'm stuck to the spot, my head feels dizzy, there is a ringing in my ears, I'm coughing the smoke out of my lungs, and when it finally starts to clear and I can see and breathe once more, I have no idea what on earth I am looking at!

Chapter Three

What Is the Worst That Can Happen?

Our plan (the one set out by Bella to stop Tammy and Charlotte from ruining our science lesson, stop them in their quest to '*shake the class up*' and stop them from ultimately getting Mrs Elliot fired from our school so that we never see her again) did not feel like it was going *exactly* as Bella had said it would.

As the grey smoke all round me completely disappears, I try to focus my fuzzy eyes on something. I forget about looking at the strange green floor underneath me and instead stare at the massive shiny brown column directly in front of me. It is tall. In fact, it just keeps on going up and up. It's also wide. It is as wide as my arms if I stretch them both out. How did it get there? Who put it there? Or more importantly, why am I suddenly standing right in front of it? No. Wait. Why is it suddenly right in front of me?

"What *am* I looking at?" I say out loud, my head feeling completely and utterly dizzy. "Am I dreaming? Have I been teleported to some far-away unknown land of strange and wondrous things? Or am I in fact—"

"Clara!" shouts a small, distant voice.

"Bella?" I shout back, turning around and then back around again, wondering where on earth her voice came from, and making myself so dizzy that I nearly fall over.

"Clara!" she shouts again, a bit louder this time.

"Bella, where are you?"

"Up here!"

Slowly, stepping back but still looking at the massive, shiny brown column in front of me, my eyes look up. I still feel completely and utterly dizzy and looking up like this really is not helping at all. Stepping back two more spaces, I carry on, my eyes going up until they reach high above me to what looks like a wooden ledge. I step back further, watching the ledge, until my fuzzy eyes see a blurry Bella standing on the very top of it waving at me with both arms above her head.

"How did you get up there?" I shout up to her. "And, where are we?" I add, wanting to shut my eyes to stop my head from spinning.

"Well," she begins to say, pausing to scratch the side of her head and then pausing some more to rub her forehead with her fist. "I'm not sure how to explain."

"What happened to our plan?" I shout, feeling very confused. "We... umm... we were going to catch Tammy and Charlotte. Catch them in the act of... No, we were going to sit and wait by the bag... weren't we?"

Bella doesn't answer me; she just smiles a very thin smile that doesn't really look like a smile. It looks more like she either has some really bad news or she has hit her toe on something hard and doesn't want anyone to know how much it hurts.

"Bella, what is that large black thing behind you?"

She turns to look at what I'm pointing at and I look at it too, as a sparkle of metal on the top of it catches my eye. Quickly an image of Bella with a wild stare on her face and with her hands reaching to open Mrs Elliot's big black bag plays, as if it was happening right in front of me at this very moment. Blinking a few times and the image goes. Instead, I notice another red thing to the other side of Bella. This has metal bars attached to it. My eyes move from the black thing to the red thing and then back again. They both look strangely and horribly familiar.

"Ummm, right, is that Harry-the-Hamster's cage next to you?" I point. "And is that Mrs Elliot's black bag right there behind you?"

Bella turns back, looks down at me and nods very slowly.

"But they look completely and utterly massive..." I start to say in reply, and then stop as the dizzy feelings in my head get so bad that I definitely have to shut my eyes while my whole brain feels like it is about to explode in some kind of gooey dizzy mess.

Last summer, Mum and Dad took my older brother Darren and me to these rides by the beach. We spent the whole morning on the beach with Granny and Grandad and then we all went on the rides. There were loads of them and they were brilliant. My favourite was the one that went up really high in the sky and then splashed down into the water underneath, absolutely covering everyone on the ride and those watching and trying to record it with their mobile phones. What I didn't like at all was this one ride that you sit in and it spins you round and round for absolutely ages. Then, when the music stops, you have to get out. That was horrible and Darren thought it was hilarious. I hated it. I couldn't walk straight and there were three of Mum standing in front of me asking me if I was OK. It took the rest of the day for the dizziness to go.

When I can open my eyes again, I look at my feet and the strange green carpet underneath them. There is a big piece of mud next to me, which is the size of the round purple rug in my bedroom. Very slowly, because my head is still spinning, I look up and out across at a room covered in tall, thin, brown shiny pillars. My eyes are still fuzzy. I blink several times and then rub them with my fists. Chair legs – the room is covered with giant chairs.

"How?" is all I can ask when I slowly look back up at Bella again. A large sick feeling has risen up from my stomach and is stuck in my throat.

"I'm sorry!" she shouts back down at me.

Sorry. I am sure that she is sorry, but at this very moment in time, as I puzzle over how and why everything has grown so massive, 'sorry' doesn't quite seem to answer my question. I puzzle over this some more as I watch Bella grip hold of the shiny brown column, that I now understand is a table leg, and gingerly lower herself down it.

"How did everything get so huge?" I ask when Bella finally reaches the bottom of the table leg. I am impressed with her brilliant climbing-down skills, but I can't think about this now. "What is going on?"

"Ah, well, there, I can answer that one," she says. "But you are not going to like it."

"I'm not?"

"No."

"Why—"

WHOOSH – BOOM!

"…What was that noise?" I manage to ask as a rush of wind blows across the room.

BOOM!

"Clara!" Bella shouts.

"Yes?"

BOOM!

"Run!"

BOOM!

"What?"

"This way, quickly!" she shouts again, grabbing my wrist and pulling me so that we run straight under the table that Bella had just been standing on.

The ground shakes underneath our feet and there is another sudden rush of wind that blows me sideways – nearly knocking me over. Bella, still holding on to my arm, pulls me along as we continue to run.

"What is going on?" I demand as we reach the wall. I watch as Bella squashes her back firmly against the wall as if she wants to melt into it. "What are you doing?"

"Shush," she whispers, her finger up to her lips before pointing directly in front of her, her eyes fixed in the same direction, causing me to turn my head.

And that's when I see them – four giant black shiny patent leather shoes with dark green tights, and they are coming towards us.

"What is that?"

"Tammy and Charlotte," Bella breathes out, the words barely making a sound.

"Tammy and Charlotte? They are huge too?" I question. "Let me get this straight – the room is huge, the chairs and tables are huge, the bag and Harry-the-Hamster's cage. Why is everything so huge?"

"Shush!" Bella says again, her eyes briefly looking at me before turning back to the patent leather shoes next to the table, her finger moving up to her closed lips. "Shush," she says again in a whisper.

"Or…" I puzzle, looking at Bella and then at Tammy and Charlotte's shoes. "Have we somehow shrunk?"

"Yes," she whispers very slowly, her hand now hovering in front of my mouth. "We *have* shrunk, and will you please be quiet because the last thing we want is for *them* to find out."

Chapter Four

Disbelief, Grief and Furious Rage

A brilliant piece of advice. Perfect, in fact. Bella was, of course, completely right – if ever you find yourself shrunk at school by an overly paranoid science teacher who specialises in chemistry, then it is best not to let the two horrible girls in your class (who seem to take joy in being mean to anyone around them and who are now GIANTS), know about it. That would be called – '*making a really, really, really bad situation even worse*'.

So, I understand why Bella looks scared, but for me, right now, I am still trying to process a lot of emotions, with the main two being disbelief and grief.

Disbelief: because I am still not entirely convinced that we haven't actually been teleported to some far-away unknown parallel universe where everyone and everything is gigantic. Or, in fact, whether I am, of course, still in bed at home, dreaming this whole day up! That could be a real possibility.

Grief: because I want to say 'why me' over and over and over again until it becomes a whole new word in the English Dictionary – **Whyme**. adv. 1. When grief over something happening to you is so completely overwhelming that you have nothing else to say. 2. A deep-down feeling that whatever is happening to you should really be happening to someone else that isn't you.

I haven't got to ABSOLUTE FURIOUS RAGE yet, but I think that really can't be far behind.

*

"There it is," Tammy's voice booms, causing the four black patent leather feet with green tights to stop in front of the table. "It's open."

"Good, hurry up," Charlotte's voice booms in reply, her black patent leather feet shuffling and moving, every step mesmerising as it lifts and lowers, my eyes caught in a hypnotic stare as I watch them.

"Alright, alright," Tammy replies.

With my mind focusing on the emotion '*grief*', for now, my ears fill up with sound-muffling cotton wool that makes the two giant voices sound like they have socks in their mouths. My eyes also keep watering from staring so hard at the giant boat-sized feet in front of me.

"Why has this happened to me – why me, why me, why me," I whisper as Charlotte's feet start to move away from the table. I can see a sticker on the bottom of her shoe, and I know that if I ran towards those patent leather feet, she could quite easily squish me and I'd be like that sticker, all squashed and stuck to the bottom of her shoe forever.

"Hey, what are you doing here?!" Charlotte yells out.

"What?!" I gasp, my lungs immediately fighting for breath as I tense my whole body. What did she say? How... what? Is this it? Is a giant hand about to grab me? Why me?!

Standing under the table, holding on to the wall behind me with both hands, my back stuck to it too, as if it will protect me or make me suddenly completely invisible, my eyes are shut, my body is tense, and instead of a hand grabbing me, I can hear another voice. A very familiar voice.

"I'm just looking for someone," the voice says from the other side of the room.

"Hey, that's Reggie," I whisper. Releasing my grip on the wall and opening my eyes, I turn to Bella. "It's Reggie! He's here to save us!"

I probably said that last part a bit too loud, really, because as I release my grip on the wall, I leap away from it, and I forget about our urgent need to be quiet. I also jump up and down and clap my hands together.

But that doesn't matter! Reggie is here to save us.

A great emotional wave of excitement and happiness at being saved from this terrible scary mess instantly replaces my complete disbelief and terrifying grief. He will save us from this devastating madness and carry us directly to Mrs Elliot, and she can make us big again. Everything solved. Reggie will save us like a knight in shining armour.

"Well," replies Charlotte, her feet now far away from the table. "There's no-one here. Everyone is at break, obviously."

"You're not."

"No."

"So, it's not everyone then."

"No, but what you going to do about it?"

"Nothing – I'm just saying."

"Well, I don't care what you're saying… Are you going to go now or not?!"

"Erm right, sure, I'll go then if it's just you here—"

"It is just me, so, like… Bye!"

There is an instant silence. I cannot hear anything.

Still full of hope, I strain my ears to hear a noise that will tell me Sir Knight Reggie hasn't gone and is actually still here. Then, not wanting to lose any tiny bit of hope, my mind starts to come up with some new ideas:

"Reggie won't believe her," I whisper, slowly moving back to hold on to the wall again. "He will save us. He'll come back… Or he'll run and get Mrs Elliot… Yes, he'll find Mrs Elliot and bring her here."

I look at Bella, but her wide eyes are still staring at the feet in front of us and the two returning feet of Charlotte. I don't think Bella has moved her head since they arrived and I'm now wondering if she has breathed at all.

"But, then again," I continue in a whisper, watching Bella for any signs of breathing. "How will he know we are here? He probably thinks we have gone to break and have abandoned our plan to stop Tammy and Charlotte in the act of ruining today's science lesson… Do you think he will try and find us?"

Bella doesn't move. She keeps completely still like a mannequin in a shop window or a stone statue in the middle of a city.

"He's not going to save us, is he? He's not going to carry us away like a knight in shining armour. He doesn't even know we are here."

My heart feels like it wants to sink to the floor. My happiness has been quickly pushed out of the way by sadness.

"That was close," Charlotte booms. "You finished yet?"

"Yeah, all done." Tammy laughs, and I notice the sound of glass hitting against glass in a small '*clink*' way.

"Good," Charlotte replies, also laughing. "Then let's go before anyone else sees us."

*

"What do you think they did?" Bella says, suddenly snapping out of her unmoving statue pose, breathing and blinking once more.

She made me jump.

I had seen Tammy and Charlotte leave, but I was too full of misery to really care. I simply kept staring at where their feet had been, my brain moving fluidly from grief and into the darker grounds of anger and rage.

"Clara?" she questions.

"I never wanted to join you," I begin, still staring out at the missing feet. "I never wanted to skip break to watch Mrs Elliot's bag, or rush my lunch, or skip the jam roly-poly. I love jam roly-poly. I didn't want you to open the bag."

"I'm sorry," Bella cuts in.

"You opened it and now look at us – we are completely and utterly tiny. And… and Reggie didn't save us! He was here, right here, and he left!"

"Yes… that would have been useful—"

"Bella," I say sharply, turning to look at her, wondering if she fully realises what is going on. "She shrank us! Mrs Elliot actually shrank us! It should be Tammy and Charlotte down here the size of a hamster, not us!"

"Yes, that is very true."

Bella is replying to my ranting a little too quickly for my liking. She's up to something, so I stop talking. I stay silent and watch her with my eyes narrowing at the sight of her jiggling on the spot with her hands clasped together in front of her. I have seen her do this before. In fact, she did this exact thing to me two weeks ago when she had asked me how my weekend was, when really she wanted to tell me that she had been to the new cookie shop in town, 'Millie's Cookies'. They had put loads of extra smarties on top because she was their first-ever customer. She was bursting to tell me and wasn't listening to anything I was saying about my swimming lesson. This is exactly what she is doing now.

Taking my silence as her turn to speak, Bella's important question bursts out of her. "What do you think they did to her bag?"

"Agh, Bella, I don't care!" I yell.

"What?"

"I don't care what they did – I didn't care before and I don't care now! We need to go and find Mrs Elliot, tell her she made a huge mistake shrinking us and get her to turn us back – preferably before home-time!"

"Yes, of course, but no, we need to work out what they did."

"Are you joking!?"

"No – did they take something or add something or worse, did they mix something?"

"I don't care! I just want to be normal size again."

"I know you do, I do too, but we hardly have any time now before the whole class comes back in and Mrs Elliot starts her lesson. If we leave, we might miss her and well, something very serious could happen and she could get fired and then there will be no more extra science lessons!"

I am absolutely stunned. She is not joking. She cares more about our science lessons than she does about being shrunk to the size of a mouse! Honestly, what is more serious?

"Then you do it," I say, watching the look of hope on Bella's face fall away. "I'm going to find Mrs Elliot and get her to turn me back. *Then* I can say that Tammy and Charlotte did something to her bag."

"Wait, Clara, what if you miss her and the lesson starts?"

"I don't care!" I shout, feeling too angry and too furious with her.

Running fast towards the slightly open door to the classroom, I ignore her calling after me and I don't look back. I have been shrunk; my precious Rule Number One: Avoid Trouble is itself in serious trouble. I need to find Mrs Elliot immediately, because my trouble Spider-man-like sense is going crazy in my ears again.

As I reach the door…

WHOOSH!

It opens wide and two feet appear. Jumping to the wall beside the door, I dart out behind them, jumping through and speedily around the corner before the door quickly closes behind me.

Chapter Five

On My Own

In the empty school corridor, I stop to breathe. A huge green plastic button torn off from a school cardigan catches my eye and I stare at it, unblinking. It is in the middle of the corridor right in front of me, with a big clump of grey dust stuck to it, and it is massive. It is the size of a dinner plate and that is all I can think about: how big it is compared to how small I am now.

She always does this to me.

"Clara, you need to care more," Bella says every time she has a new mission in her head. Striding down the corridor towards the canteen because

Mrs Webster has taken baked beans off the lunch menu and I seem to be walking with her. I'm not sure why. Do I really like baked beans that much? I think, when I'm given the choice, I prefer eating peas.

Or the time I went with her to complain because we weren't allowed outside in the snow. I mean, I like being outside, I really do, and I like it when it's snowing, but I kind of agreed with Mr Graveshead – it did look cold.

"Clara, you need to care more!" she had huffed at me.

Gritting my teeth together, I am unbelievably angry: angry with the situation Bella has put me in, angry with the fact that from the very beginning I wanted nothing to do with this plan of hers and completely angry with the very fact that I was right – she should not have opened that bag! Yet, very annoyingly, being right does not seem to be helping me here.

With a swirling storm of anger in my head I decide to run. Staying close to the wall, I make sure to avoid the hot copper pipes leading to the radiators. There is also a lot of grime and mud by the wall, which is horrible, and I never realised the floor was so dirty before and so I make sure I run around and avoid this too.

Then, it is only when I reach the first step down to what now looks like a sharp cliff face rather than the school stairs, does my head start to completely and utterly spin and I realise I really need a new plan.

New Plan:

1. Find Mrs Elliot before break finishes.
2. Tell her this has all been a big, huge mistake and can she please turn me back to my original size (but feel free to add another 5cm so that I'm finally taller than Reggie) before anyone sees me.
3. Definitely ask her to please not tell my mum and dad because this was really not my fault at all and I would really like to watch *When Nature Fights Back* on TV tonight.
4. Tell her about Tammy and Charlotte and that they probably have done something quite bad to her big black bag.

Yes, a new plan. Focus: stop dizzy head from spinning.

So, if I'm right, then the teachers either take a really long time eating their lunch very slowly or they are just hiding in the room that we are not allowed to go in or knock on the door of – 'The Staff Room'. It is a school rule. Mr Graveshead reminded us just last week. Plus he added that we shouldn't need to knock on the door as we should either be eating our own lunch or outside getting some fresh air. I nodded when he said this to the class because he was looking at me for some reason, even though I haven't ever knocked on the door. It made absolutely no sense to me at all and it really only made me think of loads of questions I wanted to ask him. I didn't put my hand up, though – mainly because Mr Graveshead shouts, a lot, and also because no-one else put their hand up so it must have made complete sense to everyone else.

I have, however, seen inside 'The Staff Room' and immediately told Bella and Reggie all about it. I was talking to Mr Whitehead at the time, who is a teacher that sometimes joins our class on a Thursday morning to read with a few of us. He's different to most of the teachers in our school as he doesn't really talk like a teacher, and so that is probably why he held the door of 'The Staff Room' wide open while he finished talking to me about a new book that I was reading. So, I got to see inside the room and it really was not that great. There was a metal sink with loads of teacups next to it, some white cupboards with one of the doors not shut properly, a round wooden table and chairs in the middle of the room, and big comfy chairs in the corner by the window. It was quite messy, really, with loads of paper everywhere and there were stacks of cardboard boxes on the floor.

Anyway, the teachers seem to like to stay in this room for the whole of lunch break, so that is probably where Mrs Elliot is right now.

Standing at the top of the stairs with the sounds of shouting and yelling from the playground outside coming from the window behind me, reminds me of my swimming lessons. It's the bit when I'm dry, I haven't got in the water yet and I'm looking down at the pool. As I stand there waiting, every voice surrounding the swimming pool echoes around the room. In fact, the first thing Claire says to us at 9:30am on a Saturday morning when we are standing next to the swimming pool is: "*Lower yourself into the pool.*"

We are not allowed to jump into the pool until later in the lesson. I know that the main reason for this is that if she told us we could all jump in straight away, then we would immediately all jump in together and that would end with us all landing on each other. I know this because Dad told me, and as soon as he said it, it made perfect sense. He is right, we would.

As I sit down on the first step, looking down at all the other steps I need to climb down if I want to reach Mrs Elliot in time, I think about these swimming lessons. Putting both my hands to one side of me, I twist towards them and lower myself down the step – just like I do to get into the pool at the beginning of my swimming lesson.

"Well, that worked well." I congratulate myself before sitting on the next step and doing the same.

And it did work well, but it was taking too long. On the fifth step, I try jumping and this is much more fun and ultimately quicker, if not exhausting, and I must remember to bend my knees before I land.

So, by the time I reach the bottom step – I lost count but there must be like twenty of them – I am exhausted and I still have to run down to the end of the corridor, past two classrooms, the girls' and boys' toilets, the doors to the playground, the entrance to the canteen and the school hall, and then turn right at the end and go past another two rooms, to reach 'The Staff Room'. And do all of this without anyone seeing me. The corridor looks huge and long, and, well, a bit scary, really.

*

Staying close to the wall again – as this feels like the safest place to be – I successfully run down the corridor without being seen. I run past the boys' toilets and the girls' toilets, and past the doors to the Reception Class. I do all of this in the quiet and empty corridor and without anyone suddenly opening a door and sending me flying through the air. Plus, I'm running with this pain in my knee from jumping the last step while also trying to hear over the sound of my own heart thumping! I can't hear anyone. I don't think there is anyone around.

A bit further, and I successfully run past both the Year 1 and Year 2 classroom doors on opposite sides of the corridor before I suddenly stop.

Standing next to the two large glass doors to the school playground, I come to a complete and utter stop. It is Reggie. It is Reggie wearing his bright yellow coat. His brilliant, bright yellow, thick, padded coat beaming out like the sun, and now that I have seen him, I can see him hopping from one foot to the other in the middle of the school playground talking to Mrs Elliot. Mrs Elliot! I don't remember Mrs Elliot *ever* standing outside at lunch break, *ever*, yet there she is, with Reggie!

"This is excellent!" I shout, jumping up and down in front of the doors with my hands on the cold glass. "I don't need to go to 'The Staff Room', she's right outside! All I need to do is get outside."

Except how am I going to get outside?

Putting a bit more effort into pushing the glass door in front of me, I try to open it. This is weird. I know the doors are a bit heavy, but usually it opens with a good push or maybe a lean and a bit of a shoulder barge. Yet the door is not opening. Not even a tiny bit.

Walking up and down in front of the glass doors, I try again to push one of them open. It is no use. I am the size of a hamster and clearly a hamster cannot open these absolutely massive heavy doors. There also doesn't seem to be any holes or any gaps near the door to squeeze through to get outside.

Putting my hands up to the glass again, I look longingly at Mrs Elliot and Reggie. Reggie is still hopping around in his bright yellow coat, his hands in his pockets with his mouth rapidly opening and closing. My brilliant plan seems to be losing its initial brilliance.

"Agggghhhhhhhh!" a high-pitched scream cries out from somewhere behind me, throwing me towards the glass door. I freeze, my face squashed up against the glass while my stomach jumps up to my throat. "Agggghhhhhhhh!" it starts again.

Instinctively, I run to my left, back the way I came, back towards the wall, looking for somewhere to hide. Where on earth do I hide!?

"Agggghhhhhhhh!" the voice screams again, much closer and louder this time, sending my head into one big thumping heartbeat as complete and utter panic takes over my whole body. Spinning around on the spot, I immediately come face to face with a block of navy-blue.

I scream, "Agggghhhhhh, what is that?"

It's a shoe. A massive, navy-blue shoe, double my size, with a humungous thick heel on it.

"Agggghhhhhh," I scream again at the shoe. I really do not want to be squished.

The shoe does not move.

Slowly backing away from the unmoving shoe, now that I have finished screaming at it, and I look up. It's Mrs Cullings! Mrs Cullings, the lunchtime teacher who usually stands outside during break-time. Wow, she is big! I didn't quite recognise her straight away with her being so close and, well, being face to face with her shoe.

"Hey, Mrs C," I start to say, waving my hands above my head. Yet, she doesn't give me a chance to finish – the massive shoe starts to move again. This time, the enormous Mrs Cullings and her huge feet start springing and leaping about all over the place. One at a time, the navy shoes are lifting high up in the air before crashing down far too close to where I'm standing.

"Hey, Mrs C," I start to say again, before quickly giving up any hope of talking to her. Her shoes are falling much too close! Screaming and throwing my hands up in the air to somehow protect my head, I run towards the wall again. The wall feels like a safe place to run to, except her left foot stamps down and blocks me! Quickly, I spin and turn around on the spot. Still waving my arms around my head, I run back to the glass door.

Mrs Cullings is screaming, I am screaming and she is most definitely leaping all around me. Her right foot falls straight in front of me, her heel almost hitting my nose, and then she lets out another high-pitched scream. “Agggghhhhhhhh!”

I am blocked. I have her giant right foot in front of me and her giant left foot stopping me from running to the wall.

“Agggghhhhhhhh!” we both scream at the same time.

“Why me, why me, why me – I’m going to get squashed!”

Acting fast, but also with a lingering fear of ending up as a sticker on the bottom of a shoe, I change direction and run straight through her legs.

CRASH!

Something pink falls right beside me, touching my leg as it hits the ground.

She’s got me! I think, before I see the pink metal

object bounce back up again, only to then fall back down to the ground.

"My glasses!" she yells. "Shoo, shoo, shoo, you horrible thing!"

Horrible thing? Horrible thing?!

Did Mrs Cullings with her giant feet just call me a '*horrible thing*'? I've always liked Mrs Cullings. She's kind. She lets you finish your apple outside and she doesn't shout when you hang on the monkey bars with just one arm. Also, if I want to sit on my favourite red bench all break-time, she doesn't tell me that I should be 'moving around' or 'being active'. I miss my red bench. Did Mrs Cullings really just call me a '*horrible thing*'?

Lifting her right foot up, she stamps it back down again so quickly that the foot just misses my bottom. Everything is happening so fast. My head is spinning, I don't know where to run to and I miss the kind Mrs Cullings. Now she is scary. She is a scary giant with massive feet who thinks I'm a horrible thing and wants to squish me!

With a sudden cold breeze on my back and the smell of the outside air, I instantly turn around to face it.

“Get out, get out, get out!” she screams, pushing wide open the glass door to the playground.

Without a second to lose, I run for the door and as soon as my feet hit the playground floor, I take an immediate right so that I can keep next to the brick wall. I then run as fast as I can until I reach the white metal shelves where we keep all the break-time play gear. Stopping here, I grab hold of the bottom shelf and hide underneath it, fighting to catch my breath as my heart pounds through my entire body and I feel like I’m going to be sick.

Chapter Six

The Plans of Mice

"Gill, are you alright?" Mrs Elliot questions as she runs across the playground towards Mrs Cullings. "I thought I heard screaming."

Mrs Cullings is bent over watching the floor. With her glasses now back on her nose and the door slowly closing behind her, she spins around and around. She hasn't moved that far away from the door. It seems that every step she takes is carefully checked, watching the floor as she spins, before she spins around again.

"No, no, no, no, no… I'm not alright," she says to the floor.

"Gill?" Mrs Elliot says, looking at Mrs Cullings and then also deciding to look at the floor. "Gill, what is it?" she says slowly.

"I just saw a mouse!"

"A mouse – where?"

"It was in the school! Can you believe it? In the school! I opened the door and it ran outside."

"Did you see where it went?"

"No, no, no, my glasses fell off. No, I can't see anything without my glasses… It was horrible!"

"Strange that a mouse was in the school. Well, I'm sure that it just got lost and it has now run off home. I bet it's far, far away by now."

Well, actually, no, not at all. I (the apparent mouse) am standing behind the white metal shelves and the break-time play gear trying to breathe again. I'm waiting for my heart to go back to its normal speed too. I feel like I can't move and that my whole body is made of jelly. That was too close and too scary. I now have a completely new respect for all mice out there in the world. In fact, I feel sorry for any small animal that is human foot-sized and easily trodden on!

Was she really trying to tread on me?

Breathe.

Breathe.

I am going to choose to believe that she wasn't and that it was just that she couldn't see anything – I can't believe she thought I was a mouse!

Past the white metal shelves, the netballs, the hoops and the plastic boxes, as I get my breath back, I can see Mrs Elliot is still talking to Mrs Cullings. Mrs Cullings bites her nail, rearranges the glasses on her nose and then ends up putting both hands on her head. "No, I don't think the mouse would have brought a disease into the school," Mrs Elliot says as Mrs Cullings twitches and turns, nods, and starts to look at the floor again. "I'm sure the children are safe," Mrs Elliot says slowly while nodding.

After two checks of the floor around her feet, Mrs Cullings stands up straight, wraps her coat very tightly around her body and nods a few times at Mrs Elliot. "Of course, of course," she repeats.

Both of them are now really just standing in front of each other, nodding at each other.

Mrs Elliot is so close to me. My cure for this terrible problem, which really was not my fault at all, is so close to me. With my breathing almost back to normal, I know it's completely now or never. I need to run over to Mrs Elliot and tell her the utterly terrible and awful news: I have been shrunk. I have been shrunk to the size of a mouse.

And I need to do it now. And it is going to be OK. It doesn't matter that just minutes ago Mrs Cullings thought I was a '*horrible thing*'. It doesn't matter that when she sees me, she might jump up and down again with her massive thick heels on. Neither of these things matter, because I am *sure* that as soon as I walk up to them both, Mrs Elliot will recognise me immediately. She will see that I am *not* furry, I *don't* have a long tail or whiskers and that I am in fact a very small version of my former self: Clara Jennings, Year 5 class. She will know exactly what has happened – mainly because she was the one who set up the trap in her bag in the first place to shrink whoever opened it – and will stop anyone from treading on me. I am *sure* of it.

"I don't think there will be any more mice, no..." Mrs Elliot says, shaking her head with big, exaggerated movements at Mrs Cullings (who has stopped looking at the floor, has stopped nodding and is again slowly wrapping her arms around herself while pulling her coat in even tighter). I am not sure she looks convinced.

As I look at them both through the shelves of the break-time play gear, the cold February air suddenly hits me, making me shiver. I jump around to warm up my freezing cold body. I know I should really be running over to the teachers now to tell them my absolutely awful news, but I'm finding it really hard to actually leave my new hiding place. One thought keeps going around and around my mind: while I *am* really sure that Mrs Elliot won't let anyone step on me, or think I'm a mouse, it would be so much easier if I had someone with me. Someone like Reggie.

It would definitely be easier to run to Reggie first, explain to him everything that has happened and then he can take me over to Mrs Elliot – just in case I do happen to look like a mouse. A mouse wearing a school uniform and walking on two legs. I check my hands immediately. No, still very much human hands.

The problem is, I'm jumping up and down and I can't see anyone sitting on my favourite red bench and I can't see his bright yellow coat anywhere.

Standing behind the shelves, I walk up and down to see if I can spot Reggie and his bright yellow coat anywhere else in the playground. How can Reggie have completely disappeared?

Walking to the furthest end of the shelves, a shadow quickly blocks out the light.

"Aghhhhh!" I scream, covering my head with my arms and falling two steps backwards.

It was a football. A GIANT football with six GIANT legs running after it – the sound of their feet hitting the playground floor like a galloping herd of horses.

"Oh my goodness, they are massive," I whisper through my hands.

Spinning around, I look through the shelves again. The running legs brought a terrifying thought to my mind: Tammy and Charlotte. It is an absolutely terrifying and chilling thought. The big Mrs Cullings was scary, sure, but the memory of Tammy and Charlotte's giant black patent leather shoes lifting up and down at the end of the table is much worse. They would *definitely* tread on me, I am sure of it, mouse-looking or Clara-looking, either way, they would do it.

"...No, they are not really pack animals, no..." I hear Mrs Elliot explaining to Mrs Cullings as I step back to my spot at the other end of the white shelving unit. With my eyes firmly fixed on Mrs Elliot now, ready to run over to her, even though I can't find Reggie but with my '*this has all been such a horrible mistake*' speech all sorted in my head, a flash of a black shoe comes to mind. The picture flashes before my eyes and stops me from running.

It's Charlotte's shoe.

Her shoes have clear sparkly gems on the outside in the shape of a flower, yet one of them, the one on her left foot, had fallen off. There was a white mark next to the flower too. I remember staring at the white mark and the missing gem while holding on to the wall, repeating my new word, '*whyme*', over and over again. Then, I saw the same white mark and missing gem again. It was when I was angry. Yes – they were the shoes that came back into the classroom as I ran out. Charlotte came back into the classroom!

Why did I not realise this at the time!?

I can't believe I didn't think about the shoes coming back into the room.

Turning away from Mrs Elliot and Mrs Cullings, with my heart beating wildly, I hold my breath. It was because I was angry and too furious to think about anything but finding Mrs Elliot, that's why.

"Oh, Bella, I'm so sorry!" I gasp, as terrible thoughts start to run through my mind. Charlotte and Tammy are really not that nice to Bella and me when we are full height, so what would they do to us if they knew we were tiny? Hopefully, Bella remained hidden when Charlotte entered the room again. "I must get to Mrs Elliot," I whisper, turning back to face the teachers again. "I've got to change us back!"

"I'd better get back in," Mrs Elliot says, her hand on Mrs Cullings' shoulder. "If you're sure you're alright?"

"Yes, yes, fine, I'm sure the mouse has gone."

"Oh, no doubt about it – off and over to a field somewhere."

"Now is my chance," I whisper. With Mrs Elliot reaching for the handle to open the glass door and Mrs Cullings bravely walking out into the playground, this is my chance. I can see them moving slowly and I count myself down from:

Three.

Two.

One. My hands are in fists at my sides like the runners I've seen on TV, my feet ready for a sprint start, my aim directly for Mrs Elliot's feet.

"Go!" I shout.

I'm off the starting blocks, running towards her; her brown boots are my destination, getting closer and closer; my feet are running faster than I've ever run in my whole entire life before this very moment in time. Until…

BAM! BOOF!

A *WHACK* to the side of my body, a split-second moment of flying through the air and then a *CRASH* as I hit the hard ground.

BOUNCE…

BOUNCE…

BOUNCE…

And the stray giant football rolls down the slope and away from my aching body lying on the floor, as I hear the sound of horses galloping after it.

Chapter Seven

Surely, Nothing Else Can Go Wrong?

There is a moment of muffled dizziness as all the different sounds from the playground around me become quiet. It's like when I'm sitting next to Darren and he has his big red headphones on but I can still hear bits of the music, just not all of it.

I stay on the floor, lying on my side, my eyes only slightly open as I watch Mrs Elliot's brown boots slide smoothly and quickly through the open door. And I want to cry. My whole body hurts and the tears are all ready and waiting in my eyes. I also want to scream. I want to scream and cry.

All of this is completely impossible! I am the size of a small rodent, and while mice and hamsters may survive this world being this small, I am clearly not going to. I'm going to get SQUISHED or SQUASHED. I can't even run across a playground without being knocked over by a stray football! I should clearly not be here with all these big giant feet and out-of-control footballs when I am the size of a mouse.

So really – and it's not *just* because I am in pain, lying on the floor of the playground hoping that no-one will tread on me – Bella was, I guess, right. She was right and I was wrong. Yes, we should have both stayed in the classroom. Yes, we should have stayed there next to the bag that shrank us and worked out what Tammy and Charlotte did to the bag, and ultimately waited there for Mrs Elliot to arrive for the lesson.

I hope Bella is OK. I hope Charlotte hasn't seen her.

I can't believe I am tiny. I can't believe I am lying on the floor of the playground, and I can't believe my aching body has sent a giant football bouncing away and down the sloping playground as it knocked me flying.

But I know this wasn't Bella's fault.

There is definitely still the fact that she should *not* have opened Mrs Elliot's big black bag. It's just that, well, she didn't *know* this would happen. Really, all along Bella's just been doing what she thought was the right thing to do to save our science lesson from complete and utter sabotage, whereas, I guess, maybe I was just trying to save myself. And now… Now I'm not sure I *can* save myself and I don't know if Bella is OK.

Sitting up very slowly, I move my hands and fingers, slowly move my feet and examine my aching leg. The sounds from the playground are getting louder and louder as my ears become less blocked, and I can feel my arms shaking as I lift them up to touch my aching head.

"What am I going to do now?" I'm stuck outside the school with Mrs Elliot now inside and Bella inside. I don't know if Bella is OK. I am the size of a mouse and let's face it – I am in BIG TROUBLE! Probably the biggest trouble, EVER!

I am still watching the empty space where Mrs Elliot's brown boots had been gliding along just moments ago and the glass door flings open again. I can't believe it; the door is opening.

"Mrs Elliot has come back!" Maybe she forgot something and has come back out to the playground. Except no – instead of Mrs Elliot's brown boot, it is a black boot. The black boot is followed by a long grey coat and it comes striding through the door, sending the coat flying all around the legs like a giant cape. "Of course, it's Mrs Regan and Miss Tully!"

Usually a bit before the bell goes, which tells us it's the end of break, Mrs Regan and Miss Tully come outside to help Mrs Cullings get everyone to tidy up the mess in the playground. It's what they say every time. Mrs Regan claps her hands together three times and says, "Right, time to tidy up this mess." It just means put everything away: footballs, hula-hoops, skipping ropes, netballs, weird dinosaur feet things that are really hard to walk on, everything, all back in the correct buckets and boxes. This is what they do every time, what they say every time, like clockwork, and this was my chance to run back inside.

Picking myself up off the ground as quickly as I can, even though there is a long stinging pain down my left arm and leg, I run. With no countdown or pausing to think or stopping or anything, I just run. I run as fast as I can with my left leg not wanting to run as fast as my right leg.

"I said, don't be funny," Mrs Regan shouts, both her feet now appearing through the doorway, with her hand opening the door wide.

I'm getting closer.

"Did you?" Miss Tully replies, walking through the doorway closely behind Mrs Regan, her red coat already tied tightly around her with its matching red belt.

"Now!" I tell myself, leaping forward and towards Mrs Regan's heels. A quick dodge to the left and I jump through and past Miss Tully's flat shoes.

"Yeah, I did," Mrs Regan says as she turns around to face Miss Tully. Except she stops. Her boots stop and this makes Miss Tully's flat shoes stop and then shuffle forwards two more steps.

I'm trapped. Four giant feet and I'm stuck next to the door – Miss Tully blocking my way into the school while Mrs Regan's black boots block me going anywhere else. Four giant feet blocking me. It's Mrs Cullings and her navy-blue shoes trying to squash me, all over again!

For a second, I freeze, just staring at the giant feet. *NO*, I shout inside my head. *I can do this! They are not going to stop me or squish me or squash me and I am not staying out here with all these footballs flying around!*

"That is so funny!" Miss Tully replies to Mrs Regan. "You should have seen his face."

Jumping back over Miss Tully's toes and then circling around to her heels, I miss what would have been a very painful kick to my bottom, as all four feet suddenly start to move again. Mrs Regan quickly turns around, Miss Tully steps to the side and they both start to walk. As fast as I can, I squeeze through between her heel and the open door, and then I turn. Throwing myself over the metal strip in the doorway and onto the scratchy mat, I land in a super stunt-like logroll on the floor.

"I wish I had! I always miss these things," I hear Miss Tully say as I keep rolling and rolling. While she lets go of the door and lets it swing back and close, both teachers seem completely unaware of the mouse in Green Grove's school uniform that has just run through their legs.

*

Standing at the glass doors, I stare out at the playground, my hands up to the cold glass as Mrs Regan and Miss Tully stroll up to Mrs Cullings. Then I remember that I need to breathe, and I gasp for air. My amazing super stunt-like log-roll was like a superhero or special agent manoeuvre, but I can't deal with any more close encounters with any more giant shoes. I breathe, watch the three teachers talking and then I turn around to face the corridor. It is time to move.

"Mrs Elliot must have gone to 'The Staff Room,'" I say to the empty corridor, backing away from the doors and looking towards it. "And I'm going this way," I whisper, looking the opposite way back towards the stairs.

I need to make sure Bella is OK. I want, so badly, to be back to my original size (with 5cm added on), but I need to get back to the classroom. I can't be chasing Mrs Elliot all break-time because Bella's right, I might miss her. I could get squashed. I could get trodden on or trapped somewhere and she could walk straight past me again. She might start the lesson without me. Then there is the fact that Tammy and Charlotte have *definitely* done something to her bag, which means they might actually '*shake the class up*' and Mrs Elliot could get fired! What was I thinking? Bella was completely right – Mrs Elliot will come to class and I can ask her to change us back then instead of all this chasing.

With the corridor still empty, I run. Keeping very close to the walls, I make only a few quick glances behind me as I head towards the stairs. It feels dangerous and scary and somehow spooky being in the corridor again. I am paranoid about being trodden on, yes. Twice I've been trapped by giant feet and it's not something I want to happen again. A pause and a quick sprint past the Year 2 and Year 1 classrooms. A stop and a quick sprint past Reception Class. A quick glance behind me, and I don't even notice the pain in my knee as I continue to run.

"HA HA HA, Mr Graveshead is going to go ballistic!" booms a familiar voice, the sound rushing down the quiet corridor and hitting me. I nearly scream.

"Tammy and Charlotte," I gasp, halting in my tracks. That voice could only be the voice of Charlotte.

"He is going to go mental and Mrs Elliot will be fired on the spot!" replies the familiar voice of Tammy as four feet with green legs turn the corner from the stairs and start walking towards me.

Immediately, without even thinking about how much it's going to hurt, I dive left headfirst and roll into the open doorway of the girls' toilets.

"I can't believe it! She's, like, done all the work for us." Tammy laughs.

Crouching down by the doorway, I stick my head out in the direction of the stairs, see a blur of green and then hide again. Even if I wanted to scream, I don't think the sound would come out. I cover my mouth with the sleeve of my jumper, just in case.

"Seriously, though, I can't believe she would, like, make someone smaller," says Tammy, as I see the massive giant feet stomp past the doorway right in front of me, heading down the corridor.

"I know – crazy, isn't it?"

Bella! I yell in my head. *They are actually talking*

about Bella! They must have found her and they know it was Mrs Elliot that shrank her!

"And you know what to say?" continues Charlotte.

"Yeah, yeah – '*She could have done this to all of us!*' I got it."

"And?"

"Oh yeah… '*She's just not safe to have in the school!*'"

"HA HA HA." Charlotte laughs again at Tammy's scarily good acting skills. "Brilliant, wait until he sees her, though, yeah?"

"Yeah, course," replies Tammy, as I hear the four feet stomp down the corridor and away from me.

Sticking my head out of the doorway to the girls' toilets again, I watch them as they turn the corner at the end of the corridor. They both start laughing again, their laughter ringing around the walls as they walk.

They are off to find Mr Graveshead. They have found Bella, they have found out that Mrs Elliot shrank her and now they are off to tell Mr Graveshead. But where is Bella? What have they done with her?!

Chapter Eight

A Steep Climb

I have to say it, climbing back up the stairs to the classroom is not as easy as jumping down them and it really is not as fun either. Both hands – reach up to the step – pull myself up onto my elbows – then onto my right knee – climb up – walk over to the next step – repeat.

Time to work out a New Plan of Action…

New Plan:

1. Find Bella.
2. Say sorry.
3. Try and work out how to avoid being seen by Mr Graveshead, Tammy and Charlotte,

and once again work out how to stop them ruining our science lesson and altogether stop Mrs Elliot from being fired.

OK, so I know I should never have left Bella in the first place and that she was right – Mrs Elliot *will* eventually come to the class to teach the lesson and we can ask her to change us back then before anyone sees us. But now the situation is even worse and this is most certainly going to get Mrs Elliot fired on the spot: Mr Graveshead finding a smaller version of Bella, and Tammy and Charlotte telling him that Mrs Elliot did it! Well, that is a good way to get us all in trouble and a great plan if you want to stop our extra science lessons altogether and get Mrs Elliot fired! Still, this is no time to compare plans or work out who has the better plan or think about how much trouble we are all in right now. This is the time to make sure nothing else can go wrong.

*

Five more steps to climb: yay! I can see the window at the top of the stairs.

Four more to go: must not think about how much my arms hurt.

Three more stairs: I can do this!

Two more: this is fine; I could carry on doing this all day.

One more: please don't let there be any more stairs; I just cannot take it anymore.

*

With my arms aching and my legs feeling OK, really, I run back down the corridor, past the giant green button on the floor, and then stop. Very slowly, I step past the door and into the Year 5 classroom.

Everything is quiet. I expected noise, a lot of noise. Mostly, I expected yelling – a kind of 'princess locked in the castle' yelling for someone to save her from the red, spiky, flame-throwing dragon. Or a few '*Help! Won't someone help me, please!*' noises. Except it is completely quiet.

"Bella?" I shout as I run forwards and into the room. "Bella!" I shout a little louder as I look into the distance through all the chair and table legs. This is really strange – why is she not replying? Did I hear Tammy and Charlotte right? I'm sure they were off to get Mr Graveshead and I'm sure they were saying 'wait until he sees her'. She must still be here.

I turn around and quickly run back to our blue class coat hooks. The place is a complete mess: PE bags, hats, single gloves, jumpers, trainers, cardigans and a few white socks all over the floor. I jump up and down, jumping to the left and then to the right, repeating Bella's name until it feels like I should probably stop.

"Where could she be?" I say to myself as I turn around to look at the classroom again.

Walking back towards the tables and chairs again, I go over to the table that has Mrs Elliot's big black bag on it. My heart sinks. I can actually feel my heart sinking with fear. I hate that bag. Well, I don't hate it; I just really don't want to go near it, or look at it, or be in the same room as it at all, ever. However, that big black bag is the only place left that I can think the horrible Tammy and Charlotte would have put Bella. Yes, an absolutely perfect place to show Mr Graveshead a very tiny Bella and to then give him their practised 'dangerous teacher' speech. I look up at the bag sitting on top of the table and I take a very big deep breath.

The funny thing about being shrunk down to the size of a mouse (I say mouse, because Mrs Cullings thought that was exactly what I was, and I am still a little hurt by the comparison, but it is nice to have something funny about being this tiny) is that I feel… lighter. I don't mean that I have suddenly lost muscle or fat or bones from my body but that I feel a little bit more… *springy*. Yes, springy. It's like I don't feel the ground is pulling me down as much as it did when I was bigger. For example, climbing up all those stairs. I mean, I do the assault courses set out by Ms Morgan in our PE class, but I am really not that great at leaping over things. Plus, on the fifth time of climbing out of the swimming pool on a Saturday morning to just jump back into the water again, my arms collapse and I'm begging Claire to please let me use the stairs. Yet, being the size of a mouse, I managed to climb up like fifty stairs (I lost count again, but I think it was fifty or probably even more). I feel springy.

So, even though this nasty big black bag did have a trap set up to shrink me, I am currently half-way up the table leg, my hands and feet gripping hold of it for dear life, and all I am really thinking about is how I am usually rubbish at climbing up the rope on Ms Morgan's assault course. If only she could see me now.

“Bella?” I ask cautiously as I reach the top of the table and walk slowly over to Mrs Elliot’s bag. “Bella?” I say again.

I’d rather not touch the bag or go much closer to it, so I say her name a little louder in the hope that maybe she will jump out of it in a ‘SURPRISE’ kind of way and be OK and safe and nothing to worry about. “Bella, can you hear me? Are you hiding? Bella, I’m sorry!”

“I’m sorry too,” a low, whispering voice says from somewhere outside of the bag.

I turn around quickly, ready to run away. I wasn’t expecting the noise and I’m feeling quite jumpy, really, and altogether very paranoid about being squashed or trapped! “Hello?”

“Clara, I’m over here,” the low, whispering voice says again, definitely outside of the bag.

“Oh phew, Bella, it is you… Where are you?”

“Shush, over here! And be quiet, we don’t want to wake up Harry.”

“Harry… Harry-the-Hamster?” I question, even more confused. “Why wouldn’t we want to wake him up?” I ask as I make my way cautiously around Mrs Elliot’s bag, following the direction of Bella’s voice.

Looking all over the table for Bella, I am starting to get a bit annoyed with this hide-and-seek game – how can it be so hard to see her when we are the same height? "Bella, where are you?"

"Clara," she replies with equal amounts of annoyance in her voice. "I am right in front of you."

"You are?"

All I can see apart from the empty table in front of me is Harry-the-Hamster's cage. I can see the metal bars, the red tray underneath, his plastic wheel, water bottle, a pile of paper shavings, and then my eyes suddenly stop.

The food bowl.

Sitting on top of a bowl full of seeds and nuts is a tied-up Bella directly in front of me.

"Wow, Tammy and Charlotte are *really* mean!"

"He's asleep," she says, nudging her head towards the large pile of paper shavings in the far corner of the cage. "Please help!"

Chapter Nine

A Nutty Distraction

"Are those elastic bands?" I say to Bella through the bars of Harry-the-Hamster's cage, pointing at the brown bands around her arms as she sits unmoving in his food bowl. "And is that a hairband around your legs?" I add, pointing at the purple band, which is as thick and as long as a rope, wrapped around her legs three times.

"Yes," she replies with a nod. "And they hurt a bit," she adds.

Harry-the-Hamster's cage is a simple cage and what I can only assume all hamster cages must look like, but then I've not seen many other cages and

I'm not allowed to even *think* about having a pet at home. That is exactly what Mum said when we were in the pet section of the garden centre, "*Don't even think about it*." I wanted a gerbil. The lady standing next to them said they come in pairs for company. Mum wrinkled her nose as we watched them running around and around the cage and then said, "*No*," very slowly.

So, like the cages in the pet section of the garden centre, Harry-the-Hamster's cage is rectangular with metal bars all round it and these bars sit inside a red plastic tray. The lid to the cage is on the top and there is a red plastic wheel attached on one side (for Harry-the-Hamster to apparently run on to get some exercise, but I've hardly ever seen him actually use it). He has a water bottle strapped next to the wheel too, newspaper right at the bottom of his cage, lots of paper shavings, cotton wool and a big brown food bowl.

Harry-the-Hamster, according to Mr Graveshead, is a typical hamster as he sleeps most of the day, but then sometimes in the afternoon he wakes up to grab a bite to eat. This basically means he:

1. Runs over to his food bowl.
2. Spends time filling up his cheeks with food so that they suddenly look massive, like a big furry scarf around his head.
3. Runs back to his bedding and hides in his pile of paper shavings and cotton wool bedding to eat his food.

*

Getting a good place for my foot on one of the horizontal bars of Harry-the-Hamster's cage, I grab one of the vertical bars and pull myself up. The plan is to enter the cage, untie Bella and then escape – all without waking up Harry-the-Hamster. Unfortunately, the only way to get Bella out is through the lid on the top of the cage. Climbing up the side of the cage, I lift myself up using the bars and pull myself onto the top of the cage. That's when I am sure I hear a noise.

Scuffle. Scuffle.

Immediately, I stop moving. I have one hand on the bar out in front of me and I have a foot stretched out behind me. I can only imagine I look like a freeze frame of Spider-man climbing across a building. Did I really hear a noise? I'm sure I can't hear any more noises now.

I look over to Bella. She's not moving, it certainly wasn't her, so I look at where Harry-the-Hamster is hiding under his paper shavings and cotton wool. I definitely cannot hear any noises. I also don't think I can hold this Spider-man position for much longer without my arms completely aching. I look back at Bella and she is watching me with a strange staring face. Her eyes are big and wide and her mouth is all wrinkled. I am guessing her look means, '*stop making so much noise and hurry up before he wakes*'. So, even though I really don't want to, I try again and crawl slowly towards the lid.

At the lid, I generally feel a bit happier because there have been no noises of any kind. I kneel down next to the lid, even though my heart is hitting my chest so hard I think I might be sick. Gripping hold of the metal catch, I pull it upwards.

TWANG!

A humungous-ly loud noise rings out to the entire room! It's not easy opening the lid of the cage and I forget it tends to make a loud noise, which seems to be even louder when you are really tiny and sitting next to it.

"Oops," I whisper. Still holding on to the lid, I look up and over to Bella again. "Sorry," I mouth, not wanting to make a sound.

Quickly, we both look over to where Harry-the-Hamster is hiding. I saw something. I'm almost completely certain that the big pile of paper shavings on top of him moved. It was quick, like a shiver, but I'm sure we both saw it. I wait, wondering if it will happen again. It doesn't move. I must have imagined it. Definitely.

The thing is, I've never been scared of Harry-the-Hamster and in fact I quite like holding him at the end of the day when we take it in turns to clean his cage out. My only issue is that last week Megan was sitting down and he was running from one of her hands to the other while Craig cleaned out the cage, and Harry-the-Hamster actually bit her. It was just a little bite and there was a little bit of blood, but Mr Graveshead was not happy at all. Surprisingly, he was not upset with Harry-the-Hamster but with the rest of us, and said that if we can't learn to hold him properly, then we won't be allowed to hold him, ever. Mr Graveshead was really angry. More angry than normal.

So, it's not that I am scared of Harry-the-Hamster; it's just that now I am the same size as him and I am a little bit worried about his long, sharp teeth. I didn't see him bite Megan, but perhaps (it occurs to me as I prepare to enter his cage) he might not like us in his cage with him or like having us anywhere near his precious brown food bowl.

I take a deep breath, watching to make certain that the pile of paper shavings covering him is definitely not moving, or shivering at all, and then I lower myself quickly down into the cage and drop to the ground with perfectly bent knees.

Through the floor covered in paper shavings (and a lot of rather large poo), I get to Bella and the food bowl. Bella has her arms behind her back, with an elastic band around her wrists, which also covers her hands, one around the top of her arms and a purple hairband around her legs.

I shake my head. "Tammy and Charlotte are so mean."

Time to move quickly. Starting with her hands, I pull off the tightly wrapped elastic band that seems to just keep going and going and going. Then, putting the band under my arm so that I don't leave it in the cage, I move straight on to her arms.

Crunch – crunch – crunch.

There is a sound coming from behind me. As soon as I hear it, I freeze on the spot. Bella twists her head to look around at where I'm standing. She looks past me and I stay completely still. I close my eyes. If I close my eyes the noise might stop.

Crunch – crunch – crunch.

Very slowly, still holding on to the elastic band around Bella's arms, I open my eyes and turn my head to look over my shoulder. There's that sick feeling again.

Crunch – crunch.

It's Harry-the-Hamster.

Crunch – crunch.

He is standing next to his pile of paper shavings holding on to the end of a lettuce leaf. I can see his long, white whiskers and orange head with his deep black eyes looking straight at me – and…

HE IS HUGE!

I cannot get over how huge he is. As he catches me watching him and his sharp claws gripping hold of his lettuce, he stops chewing and just stares at me. I freeze and stand completely unmoving as the words, *He is huge*, are repeated over and over in my head. Harry-the-Hamster freezes too. There is a large single piece of white curly paper shaving on the top of his head that wobbles a bit but ultimately sits there too, not moving. No-one is moving at all. Someone needs to move.

Unfreezing my body, but with my eyes still definitely looking at Harry-the-Hamster, and with no sudden or alarming movements, I take the last loop of elastic band over Bella's head. Then, still moving very slowly, I work my way around to the other side of Bella and the food bowl. Bella then uses her free hands to help wriggle her legs out of the hairband and then gently slides off the food bowl to stand next to me. This whole thing is done so slowly that it could easily be one of those slow-motion cameras they use at the end of a really close race to work out who the winner was.

We are now both standing very still as we face Harry-the-Hamster, his food bowl in-between us, neither of us moving. We watch him and he watches us.

"What do we do?" I whisper out of the corner of my mouth, wondering how much time we have left before Harry-the-Hamster does decide to move.

"Get out of here," Bella replies, still standing stock still next to me, her mouth hardly opening to speak.

As if he can understand us and everything we are saying, Harry-the-Hamster drops his lettuce leaf and places his claws down on the ground. The single piece of paper shaving that has been balancing on the top of his head tips and falls to the side.

I think fast. Grabbing the sunflower seed directly in front of me from the food bowl, I throw it as gently as I can towards his feet. He looks down at it and then up at us again with obvious disinterest in the seed. Great, now he decides he is full and doesn't want sunflower seeds.

"What now?" Bella asks.

"The nuts," I whisper, spotting them in his bowl. Harry-the-Hamster *loves* peanuts. Reaching over to pick one up, I hold it in both hands in front of me.

"Stand behind me," I say to Bella. "And see if you can jump up to get out," I add, keeping my eyes on Harry-the-Hamster but nudging with my head to get her to look up at the open lid above us.

"Are you sure?"

"Yes," I reply, watching his growing curiosity. "Jump!"

As Bella jumps, I shout, "Harry-the-Hamster!" Partly because I am wondering if he can understand me but mainly because I'm trying to get him to look at me and not at Bella leaving his cage. I lift the peanut up a bit to show him the treasure and then I throw it. The peanut flies up in the air and then falls down by his feet. "Yes!" I celebrate, watching his eyes move to the nut and then back at me.

I can feel my heart thumping in my chest – it's my turn.

Moving around to the side of the food bowl, I casually grab hold of the next peanut. Taking a quick look at the open lid, I test the weight of the peanut in my hands as I prepare to throw it.

This time I throw the nut long with my aim being the back of the cage. Up in the air and the peanut flies past Harry-the-Hamster, his eyes continually following it, as I, without a moment to lose, jump up to the roof and grab hold of the bars. My legs are dangling down. My hands grip hold of the side of the cage but they feel hot and sweaty and my grip starts to slip.

"No, I don't want to be hamster food!"

Digging my elbows into the gaps in the metal bars, I heave myself up and onto my stomach. Bella is already starting to close the lid as I drag my legs up and onto the roof. I can see Harry-the-Hamster. He has abandoned his interest in the thrown peanut and is scurrying over to where we had been standing. He looks around his food bowl and then up at us as the lid comes down, safely shutting him inside the cage.

Chapter Ten

Our Mission

I'm watching Harry-the-Hamster on the other side of the metal bars as he suspiciously examines one of the peanuts I threw for him. As I watch him, my heart gently slows down from its rapid pounding to what feels like a normal beat. I have kind of forgotten what a normal heartbeat feels like. I feel a little less shaky, the sick feeling has gone too, and being this side of the cage rather than in the cage with him feels completely and utterly less scary.

Remembering to breathe, I take a deep breath and watch as he decides that the peanut might still be OK. He carefully picks it up, stuffs it into his cheeks and then looks around for more.

"Harry-the-Hamster is the size of a brown bear," Bella says as she stands next to me, breaking the silence in the room and startling him. He looks at us, quickly abandons any intentions to find more nuts and runs off with his food-stuffed cheeks to hide under his pile of paper shavings.

"Yes." I nod, remembering too the book we were both looking at last month in the library on identifying grizzly bears versus black bears. Harry-the-Hamster is definitely the size of a brown grizzly bear. "That felt… close," I reply, still wondering if he would really have hurt us. "Tammy and Charlotte are *really* mean."

"Charlotte!" Bella breathes as she spins around to face me. "She… she was over by the sink!"

I look at Bella's horrified face and then past her to where the sink is, which is just slightly around the corner from us, by the door and opposite the entrance to the blue class coat hooks. "She went to the sink?"

"Yes, you left and then she came in – she went straight to the sink. I heard her and I wanted to see what she was doing. That's when she caught me—"

"I'm sorry," I say. "I should not have left."

"Um, yeah, well, I guess if you hadn't left then we might both have got caught," she replies awkwardly. There is a weird uncertainty in her voice that makes me think she doesn't really mean what she's saying; she's just being nice because I came back and I rescued her from the grizzly brown bear.

"So, we should look at the sink," I say, making my way to the edge of the table, leaving Harry-the-Hamster to eat his snack.

"And, I'm guessing you didn't find Mrs Elliot—" begins Bella as she watches me easing myself off the table, ready to climb down the table leg.

"No," I interrupt, starting my descent. "It's really not very easy running around school when you are the size of a mouse."

"A mouse?"

"Yeah, a mouse."

*

Bella and I stand in front of the huge cream cupboard doors and look up high above us to a point where we know the sink is, if only we could see it. I'm standing in a large stain of dried-out blue paint that has been on the floor in front of the sink for as long as we have been in Year 5 class. The cream door in front of me has the remains of something red on it too that has been washed but has left its mark all the way down the door, like a long drip.

"How do we get up there?" I puzzle. Bella and I are still looking up to the top of the cupboard like tourists looking up at a skyscraper in the middle of an abandoned city.

"A chair!" Bella exclaims, immediately running off to the nearest chair leg. "We can use a chair! Come on," she urges me.

"Really?" I reply, not feeling very hopeful about this idea.

When I arrive to stand next to Bella, she is already attempting to move the chair on her own. She slightly lifts one of the front chair legs and pulls it, but the other three legs refuse to move.

"You are forgetting that we are the size of a hamster," I protest.

Bella stops, lets out a really long breath and then looks at me, jutting her jaw out and placing her hands on her hips.

"…But," I continue before she has a chance to say anything, "I could move one of the other legs at the same time and that might help."

The lucky thing is, and again, it is good to have some luck when you are placed in what can only be described as 'a very unlucky situation', is that the chairs at our school are plastic. The legs are metal, sure, but a really light, thin metal and they are hollow. The seat is then plastic and altogether they are very light and, well, quite easy to tip over.

"FOUR LEGS ON THE FLOOR!" Mr Graveshead shouts at us if we rock our chairs backwards and start balancing on two legs.

"OK, on the count of three," I shout at Bella, "we lift and pull, right?"

"Right, OK," Bella agrees as she, for a second time, grabs hold of the chair leg next to her.

"Wait!" I shout again.

"What?"

"I'm thinking," I begin, standing up straight and abandoning my chair leg, "that instead of me picking up this leg at the front next to you, that I take this leg behind me at the back…"

"Yeah…"

"...And you stay across from me at the front, then we might have a better chance of moving it – a kind of evening-out-the-load type thing."

Bella opens her mouth to speak, closes it again, tilts her head to the side and then says, "That's actually a really good idea."

"Thanks," I reply, feeling quite proud of myself, but then slightly confused as to why she seemed so shocked I should have a good idea.

"Right," I shout again, once I have changed chair legs. "One... two... three!" I yell.

Lifting my chair leg and carrying it along for a good six steps, we are actually moving the chair closer to the sink. The chair tips and wobbles, and it is heavy, so we move three more steps before we both drop it back down again.

Out of breath and after a moment's pause, I shout, "Ready again."

"Let's do it!" Bella shouts back, while gripping hold of her chair leg, her knees bent and ready to go.

"One, two, three," I say, quicker this time, and we both lift and pull our chair legs, moving the chair closer and closer towards the cupboard doors underneath the sink.

I am exhausted. By the time we get the chair over to the sink, I just want to sit and rest for a bit, but Bella immediately starts to climb up. I can only think that it must be her need to find out the truth that is keeping her going. And I get it. From the very beginning, Tammy and Charlotte have been ahead of us. Their plans have been much better and, well, their luck has been so much better too. Yes, at no point today have either of them been:

1. Shrunk.
2. Had someone try and stand on them.
3. Knocked over by a giant football.
4. Tied up and shut in a hamster cage.
5. Confronted by a hamster.

Yes, it was about time their lucky winning streak ended. Bella and I are on a mission to save our science lesson with Mrs Elliot, to stop them in their quest to '*shake the class up*' and to save Mrs Elliot from ultimately being fired so we never see her again.

I get it now and it feels good. It feels good to be on a mission to save something – to be doing something for someone instead of just sitting and watching the world go by… even if it gets us into…

into… trouble… possibly quite big trouble.

"If I stand on your shoulders, I could reach the top of the door and then get up onto the side," Bella says to me as I try to lift myself up from the chair leg and crawl onto the brown plastic seat. She looks down at me, wrinkles her forehead, her head sinking into her shoulders with a kind of hopeful lopsided smile. So, I nod, get up off my knees and move to the edge of the seat. We are on a mission.

"I'll lean down and pull you up," she adds as she lifts herself up on to the side from balancing on my shoulders before disappearing. The next second she is back, her head, then her arms, appearing over the side, her body lying completely flat, sliding herself off the side, with her right arm down ready to grab my wrist.

We are on a mission and… We. Will. Not. Fail.

Chapter Eleven

A Pink Plastic Cup

"What is all this fuss about?" a voice booms from the other side of the classroom door.

Bella and I are standing on the grey metal draining board of the classroom sink. Five seconds ago, I walked round a big wet blob of white gloopy glue while stopping a deep temptation inside of me to touch it or stick my shoe in it.

"It's glue," I said out loud and to myself. "Don't you think you're in enough trouble without getting stuck in glue?"

Bella laughed at me. It was a laugh with a big smile showing all her teeth that made me want to laugh too. This was until we heard Mr Graveshead's deafening voice, and then her smile vanished. "Run!"

"This had better be good!" Mr Graveshead shouted again as the door flung open wide.

Grabbing hold of my wrist and almost knocking me over, Bella runs. She drags me over to the tall pink plastic cup by the taps. It is the pink plastic cup that has lots of paintbrushes inside of it and the one that is always next to the sink in our classroom. We jump behind it.

"We would not have interrupted your lunch break had it not been major urgent," Charlotte replies.

"Really?!" I whisper, rolling my eyes at her fake concern. Turning to look at Bella, I see her cheeks turning a deep red.

"Well, what is it then?" he questions, sounding in a hurry to get this over with.

"She's in Harry's cage," Charlotte replies, as she, Tammy and Mr Graveshead walk past the sink, around the corner and over to Harry-the-Hamster's cage. As they move, Bella moves too. I follow her lead as she slowly side-steps around the plastic cup while they walk past us, so that we are away from them and still hidden. We huddle together and get as close as we can to the cup – for added protection.

"Who is? I can't see anything," Mr Graveshead replies. His voice sounds kind of worried. It is wobbly and angry and concerned, which is strange, as I've never heard him like this before. It makes me feel instantly guilty.

"Bella," replies Charlotte. "She's in the… What? Wait, I…"

There is a pause and then, as I keep close to the pink plastic cup for protection, I hear the familiar metal *TWANG* sound of the lid on Harry-the-Hamsters's cage opening.

"What are you doing?!" asks Mr Graveshead.

"She was right here!"

"Who was?"

"Bella!"

"In Harry's cage?"

"Yes!"

"Bella *Lewis* was in Harry's cage?"

"Yes!"

"Bella Lewis, who is about this height, had miraculously managed to squeeze into Harry's cage—"

"Yes!"

"I'll find her," Tammy's voice jumps in. "Urgh, I've got poo on my hand!"

"What is going on with you two?"

"I've got hamster poo on my hand!"

"No, not that," Mr Graveshead mutters. "I mean about Bella... Look, Tammy, will you just go and wash your hands!"

I turn to look at Bella. "Oh no, she's coming over here."

"Oh no," Bella mouths back at me, her forehead creased and sweaty.

"Bella was all small-like," I hear Charlotte saying as I slowly move away from the cup. Peering my head very slowly round the side of the cup, I need to look. For a second there is nothing and then GREEN UNIFORM. I see a big mass of green uniform coming towards us in a big fuzzy mess because I'm so scared and my eyes cannot focus.

Bella nudges my arm. "Move this way," she mouths and then points.

With tiny shuffling steps, we move back around the cup again, squeezing together, not really wanting to move too much because Mr Graveshead might see us one side and also not wanting Tammy, who's heading for the other side of the cup, to see us either. Ignoring the '*why me*' that has started to repeat itself in my head as well as TROUBLE being shouted too, I hug the cup as tightly as I can. I am hoping that in some way the cup might magically absorb me into it.

"Yeah, she was like the size of Harry!" Tammy shouts, her voice unbelievably close and ringing right through me. I imagine this is what it would be like if dinosaurs were still alive or brought back to life and I was hiding from a Giganotosaurus. Tammy shouting is like a Giganotosaurus with its roar sending a wave of fear down my spine.

Tammy is at the sink. I know she is. I can sense her standing there even though she has suddenly gone very quiet. I want to hide my face in a kind of 'I can't see you, so you can't see me' way, but I need to look. I look and I watch as the giant hand appears and reaches towards the box of handwash fixed to the wall. I watch as a big blue blob falls down onto her open massive hand before both hands disappear. My bulging eyes keep staring where the hands had been as I hear the sound of the water starting to pour out the taps. The water hits the metal sink and I feel Bella flinch next to me.

The seconds that it takes Tammy to wash the soap off her hands stretch out for like an hour. My heart is thumping so much in my throat that I feel like I'm going to choke. I can't breathe. I can't look at Bella as neither of us can move from our frozen tightly squeezed spot in the middle of being seen by Mr Graveshead or being seen by Giganotosaurus Tammy.

"Yeah, exactly," I hear Charlotte saying as the water stops pouring out of the tap. "Bella was the size of a hamster and we were so worried that we wanted to keep her safe while we found you. It was Mrs Elliot who did it!"

"Mrs Elliot?"

"It was, honest," Tammy shouts, still dangerously close to the sink and to our hiding spot.

I'm not sure I can keep frozen to the spot for much longer. My mind is going completely mad. I have visions of the three of them standing at the sink. I can imagine Charlotte wandering over to join Tammy and the both of them standing there so close to us. I can imagine Mr Graveshead coming over too and all three of them standing right there on that very spot for an impossibly long time.

I need to run. I need to move. I need to get out of here! What if they catch us?

"To be honest, like—" Tammy starts to say.

"AGHHHH!"

It was me. I made the screaming noise.

I know it came out of my mouth. I had been frozen for too long with my whole body tense as I hugged the cup for protection. My heart had been thumping the hardest it has ever thumped in my whole entire life for way too long. It was all too much. So, when a huge drop of cold water came flying through the air and landed on my back, I thought that was it! I jumped, I panicked, I thought I had been found and our whole plan had come to an end.

Actually, it was probably just Tammy shaking her wet hands all over the place.

"What was that?!" Tammy says and I immediately put my trembling hands over my mouth to stop any more uncontrollable screams coming out. My back feels cold and wet.

"What was what?!" Mr Graveshead asks.

"I thought I heard something, like a squeak or something."

"My goodness, it was probably Harry!" Mr Graveshead yells. "This is enough..."

TWANG!

"...You two have been rooting through his cage and scaring him!"

"No, wait, Bella was all small," Charlotte interrupts. "It was Mrs Elliot, she had made her all small and she was here and..."

"...and she has escaped, but we can find her," finishes Tammy.

"Yes!" shouts Charlotte.

Even though I still have my hands over my mouth, I look around the cup. Tammy is walking back to the others by Harry-the-Hamster's cage. She shakes her hands two more times and the drops fly all around her. I look back at Bella; the colour has faded from her skin and I bet she is imagining Tammy as a Giganotosaurus too. I remove my hands that have been stuck to my mouth. "I'm sorry," I say to Bella.

"Look, Charlotte," Mr Graveshead says calmly. "I think this is enough now... Can you get up off the floor? Charlotte?"

"I know I can find her!"

"Charlotte," he says again in a slow calm voice. "I know things at home have been a bit bumpy."

"What?!"

"And I know you find science hard—"

"Mrs Elliot shrank Bella!"

"She did, Mr Graveshead, honest," Tammy says, jumping in. "And to be honest, like, we are just worried about the safety of the whole class. I mean, Mrs Elliot is not safe to have in the school."

As Tammy's last words linger in the air, there is a silence in the room. It feels like it goes on for an incredibly long time. I look at Bella. Her eyes are wide and I'm wondering if she has stopped breathing again. I wonder this as I try to listen for any sounds coming from the other side of the room. Nothing. Does he believe them? Could he actually be thinking that Mrs Elliot is not safe to have in the school?

Straining my ears to hear something, anything, that might tell me what the three of them are doing, I nearly fall over when Mr Graveshead starts to speak again. "Really, right," he says at last, his voice low and slow, like a great big exhausted sigh. "Well, thank you for the complete waste of time, you can both have your own waste of time in detention on Friday."

"No, wait," Charlotte protests.

"Detention? But we were just trying to save—"

"Detention on Friday. Extra science, I think. Now go line up outside in the playground with the others."

"I know you're in here, Bella!" Charlotte shouts, her voice moving towards us. We shuffle in close, squeezing into the cup again, and Bella closes her eyes too. I hide my head. This time I definitely won't be looking at all. If Tammy has the roar of a Giganotosaurus then Charlotte would be a Spinosaurus or a Tyrannosaurus rex.

"The door! Out!" Mr Graveshead shouts.

*

Mr Graveshead is definitely still standing in the classroom. Standing somewhere in the room and being really quiet. Is he trying to look for Bella? I can't hear anything. I can hear my heart still beating in my ears and I can hear Harry-the-Hamster. It sounds like he has decided to try out his squeaky hamster wheel, if only for a really short run. I can't hear Mr Graveshead, though.

TWANG!

The lid to the cage has been opened again.

"A student in your cage," Mr Graveshead finally says, an unusual chuckle in his voice. "Hello, my little fluff-ball. How are you doing?"

Bella releases her grip on the cup and looks at me. "What? Fluff-ball?" she whispers.

I shrug – I'm confused too.

"Now, that would be funny," he continues. "Although, I can't imagine you liking that very much, hey, my boy?"

"My boy?" I repeat to Bella.

And Bella smiles. It starts as a twitch in the corner of her mouth before a full grin appears. The colour has returned to her face and she looks at me with this massive grin.

"I don't get it," I mouth at her.

Her hands fly up to cover her mouth and her shoulders start shaking. She is laughing. She is actually laughing. I'm still completely confused. '*My boy*' – I have never heard Mr Graveshead speak to Harry-the-Hamster like this, or anyone like this, ever. Mr Graveshead shouts. Now, he sounds like he is speaking in that special weird voice adults use when they are talking to babies.

"Are you hungry? Do you want me to get you some grapes?" he starts again in his talking-to-a-baby voice. "I bet you do! I bet you do. Alright then, I'll go and get you some... maybe just a couple, you do look a little spooked by something, don't you, fluff-ball?"

"Fluff-ball," I whisper to Bella, shaking my head at the craziness of hearing Mr Graveshead's secret name for Harry-the-Hamster. I watch Bella as she completely covers her whole face with her hands, her shoulders still shaking as she tries not to laugh out loud.

"Hey, now that's strange," Mr Graveshead starts to say. "What is that in your cage? A hairband. Why is there a hairband in your cage?"

Oops.

"What have those kids been up to?"

Chapter Twelve

Down the Sink

"Salt?" I say, turning to Bella for confirmation. "It looks like salt crystals," I ponder as Bella and I lean over the side, looking at the clear crystals in the corner of the sink.

Luckily, Tammy failed to clean any of the sink when she washed her hands. She left a blue blob of handwash next to the plughole, a puddle of water on the draining board and then, in the far corner of the sink, she left a definite clump of clear crystals.

"It could be lots of things," Bella replies.

"Really, could it?"

"Yeah, the salt that we put on our chips is made of sodium and chloride ions, but there are salts that we wouldn't eat. Plus, Mum puts this stuff on all the plants in the garden and that looks a lot like usual salt, but it's not and you definitely do not want to eat it."

"Oh..."

"So, really, we need to question why she is throwing away what *looks* to be sodium chloride down the sink," continues Bella.

"Because she took it out of Mrs Elliot's bag?"

"Yeah, maybe. Or she took it out of her bag and then replaced it with something else?"

I clap my hands together. "Oh! She took it out of the bag and then replaced it with something that looks very similar, but it is a completely different chemical!"

Turning away from Bella and listening to the silence in the room, I look at the clump of crystals in the sink and then sit down on the side. Watching the crystals, I let my feet swing forwards and listen to the sound it makes as my heels hit the side of the metal sink. Bella sits down next to me. "That could be really bad. We don't know what it will do if it's mixed with another chemical," she adds.

“Kind of bizarre, though, isn’t it?” I say. “I mean, neither of them know what we are learning today.”

“No, that’s true…”

“So, if they don’t know what Mrs Elliot is going to show us, but they *definitely* know it’s going to be chemistry, because we were told in the last lesson—”

“…AND she said she was going to show us a really cool experiment!” Bella interrupts.

“Right, so, they know we are going to do chemistry today and they know Mrs Elliot is going to show us a really cool experiment, but it seems strange to only replace one chemical in the bag. How would they know what chemical Mrs Elliot will use?”

Bella looks at me, opens her mouth like she’s about to say something, closes her mouth, takes a big breath and then turns back to look at the crystals.

“I think,” I say slowly, “what we *really* need to think about is – what would someone, anyone, do if they knew Mrs Elliot was going to show the class a cool chemistry experiment, but they didn’t want that experiment to go well? Like, if they wanted that experiment to go so badly wrong that it ‘*shakes the class up*’?”

Looking away from the crystals in the corner of the sink and down at her hands, Bella doesn't answer my question. There is a silence as neither of us say anything. Sitting on the edge of the sink, I listen to the sound of my feet kicking the metal basin again as I look at the blue blob of handwash and then over to the salt-looking crystals in the corner.

Bella takes a deep breath. "I guess that person would mess with *all* of the ingredients in her bag," she says calmly.

I don't immediately reply to Bella but instead I stop kicking the sink with my swinging feet. *Mess with all the ingredients.* The words repeat in my head as images of every experiment Mrs Elliot has ever shown us play in my mind. There could be some serious damage about to happen.

Taking a big breath of air too, I let the sick feeling that has risen up to my throat go back down to my stomach again. "Yeah, probably just mess with everything," I say.

*

New Plan:

1. Climb into Mrs Elliot's big black bag.
2. Try and work out what Tammy and Charlotte messed with or added or generally what they did in their attempt to '*shake the class up*'.

"Are you sure this is the best plan?" I ask Bella in the hope that there might be another plan that maybe we should consider. Perhaps a 'Plan B' that doesn't involve us going anywhere near that horrible bag that shrank us, or anywhere near any chemicals at all.

"This is the only way," Bella replies, as she walks away from me, around the blob of gloopy glue and over to where she can climb back down to our chair.

Bella was, of course, right. Plus, from my calculations, Mr Graveshead will be back really soon with those grapes for Harry-the-Hamster – unless he has completely forgotten or just brings them up later. I am really hoping that he is *not* planning on sitting in our lesson this week with Mrs Elliot and will actually be somewhere else entirely. Anyway, Mr Graveshead or no Mr Graveshead, Mrs Elliot will be here soon to teach our lesson and following behind her will be the entire Year 5 class! I am not happy about this new plan, but then again, what better place to hide from them all than in the bag that shrank us in the first place?

The shiny metal Malteser-like clasp on Mrs Elliot's big black bag is open wide. I can see it as I walk across the room from climbing down the chair, and I can see it as I get closer to the table and over to the table leg. Out of breath, tired and exhausted, I reach the top of the table and walk over to it. Once again I am standing next to Mrs Elliot's big black bag.

Holding on to the leather handle as it hangs down the side of the bag, I pull myself up. I feel like one of those gymnasts on TV that I watch with Mum. With two hands on the strap, I lift myself up and onto my knee. Once up and standing, I start to climb up the handle with my feet turned out like I'm walking on a balance beam but with my hands still holding onto the strap as I climb. Then, reaching the top of the handle, feeling a little wobbly, I grip hold of the opening to the bag and peer inside. I'm scared. I did all this without really thinking about how completely scared I am.

As I watched Bella doing the same gymnastic routine a few seconds before me, I thought, *I can't do this!* Then I saw Bella reach the top and I realised that I've got to do this. Plus, she will be in there waiting for me. Then, just as I started to think about how this looks like something gymnasts on the TV do, and how I might ask Mum if I can join gymnastics club after school, I thought about how silly it was for me to be scared. Silly, because the bag has already shrunk me, what more can it do?

Then again, perhaps I'm not being silly to be worried and my fears are actually highly justified seeing as it's no ordinary bag but Mrs Elliot's booby-trapped big black bag. Maybe it could do a lot more than just shrink me!

Slipping past the shiny metal Malteser-like clasp and climbing down into the bag next to Bella, I stop and stare in amazement. Strapped to the sides in individual dark purple holders are four neat rows of clear glass tubes with grey lids, all full of different powders, crystals and liquid substances – on both sides of the bag. Bella and I stand next to each other, turning our heads in wonder at the sight of them all.

"Twenty-eight tubes," Bella says, still looking up at them all.

"Nothing really looks obviously out of place," I reply. "And the chemicals all look different... well, a lot of them look the same, I guess," I add as I move from my spot and try to walk across the bag without touching any of the glass tubes.

Under our feet are neat piles of clear plastic petri dishes with lids, small metal spatulas, six plastic measuring cylinders, a little pile of clear glass rectangles in a clear plastic box – which I remember Mrs Elliot using before by putting a small dollop of liquid on the glass rectangle before putting it under a microscope – and there are a bunch of pipettes and glass rods strapped to the end of the bag.

"I just don't know," Bella says, shaking her head while she looks at all the glass tubes, her forehead wrinkled while she bites her bottom lip. "Swapped something? Replaced something? Or, crazy, I know, but maybe added something to each tube?"

"That does sound crazy!" I reply, and suddenly I'm feeling very worried that we have chosen to stand in a bag full of different chemicals without knowing exactly what Tammy and Charlotte did to them. I run my eyes quickly over the different tubes again. There is no fizzing or bubbling or anything that looks like it is about to explode, and I can't see any snake tongue-like flames trying to escape from any of them. In fact, it all looks very calm and still. "Tammy and Charlotte could have swapped a few labels," I add. "And thrown the salt away because they didn't need it anymore—"

"*And* added their own ingredient to the mixture?"

"Oh, maybe!" I say, now really confused.

"What do we do?" Bella questions, a shaky panic in her voice. She looks at me, her eyes unblinking, and I can sense she is waiting for me to say something to solve the problem.

Taking a deep breath, I look back at my shrunken friend as we stand in Mrs Elliot's bag. Surrounded by tubes full of chemicals, knowing that somehow Tammy and Charlotte have done something that will '*shake the class up*', I say in my best confident voice, "We do the only thing we can do: we warn Mrs Elliot."

Chapter Thirteen

A Sticky Situation

"It is *not* going to be easy to warn Mrs Elliot that we are in here and that she must *not* use any of the chemicals, without letting any of the class and especially Mr Graveshead know – that would be really bad, worse, yes, definitely worse, especially him, he must not know we are here and have been shrunk, right – so none of them must know that we have been shrunk and that Tammy and Charlotte were right, while we warn Mrs Elliot that we are in here..."

It's Bella. She is doing her 'speaking in one very long sentence with no space for breaths' thing. We are still standing in Mrs Elliot's big black bag, and since my confident decision that the only thing left for us to do is to warn Mrs Elliot, Bella has not stopped talking.

"…without letting anyone else know, we need to warn her, so she must hear us but no-one else hear us at all."

Bella finally breathes and I jump in quick: "What would you do if you didn't have a label?"

"What?" she says, pausing to look at me, her head tipping to one side. My ultra-cryptic question has worked – she looks completely baffled. "If I didn't have a label?"

"Well, I mean, what would you do if you had a tube of clear crystals and you weren't sure if it was sodium… umm…"

"…sodium chloride…"

"…Yes, salt. So, you have a tube of what looks like normal regular salt and the tube has no label."

"If it didn't have a label on the tube…" she ponders, tilting her head to the other side.

"Yes," I confirm. "A tube of stuff, any kind of stuff, and no label on it."

"Clara!" she yells unexpectedly while flinging

her arms up in the air. "That's genius! Of course."

"Thank you."

"No, really!"

I smile a huge grin and note that this is the second time today that I have come up with an idea that has caused Bella to look shocked and also amazed. I'm not sure how I feel about this. It does feel good and kind of awesome to have a great idea and then also part of me wonders why this is so completely shocking.

Following Bella's gaze, I look up at the very neat white labels with black printed text on the tubes all around us. "If the labels were not on the tubes," Bella says slowly, "then Mrs Elliot would *have* to identify the chemical using its physical properties – colour, odour..."

"...and she'll know instantly that her bag has been tampered with," I add, rubbing my hands together.

"Yes, as soon as she sees that all her labels have gone missing, she'll know something is definitely wrong."

"Then we should get started, because we really need to be quick."

With the light coming in from the top of the open bag, Bella and I take a side each. I face my first glass tube, a white powder with the neat printed label reading 'Tartaric Acid' on it. Starting in the corner, I carefully peel the label from the tube and immediately I realise that this is not going to be as easy as I thought it was. Firstly, as I am the size of a hamster, the labels are like the size of a duvet. Secondly, as soon as I manage to peel the label off, it instantly wants to wrap itself around me in a great big sticky hug. I try and peel a bit off my arm and the other bit sticks to my leg. I kick it off my leg and it wraps around my arm. I take it off my arm whilst making sure my leg is out the way and it sticks to my head! I am having an actual fight with a sticky duvet and it's like trying to get out of bed in the morning.

"Clara, stop messing around – we need to be quick, remember?" Bella scolds as I struggle to get out of the tight hold of my sticky duvet whilst peeling it off my hair. I ignore her, too frustrated with the annoying stickiness to reply. Then, when I finally manage to kick my foot away, leap onto the label before it can grab me again and wrap it into a ball, I realise that Bella is already on her third glass tube.

I really do need to move quickly, though. For our plan to work, all the labels must be completely removed because we don't know what chemicals Mrs Elliot will reach into her bag to grab. There are a lot of labels, only two of us, and there is no mistaking the sounds coming from outside of the door – voices, feet rushing up the stairs and stomping down the corridor. With everyone in from break, they are rushing to stand outside their different classroom doors. They will all be lining up and waiting. Mrs Elliot will be strolling down the corridor before standing at the very front of the queue to this very room.

I can feel my hands shaking as I begin to work on my second row of tubes. I'm standing on the lids of the first row of tubes with all the successfully peeled off labels from that row in a ball on the floor of the bag below me. I think I'm finally getting good at this. The technique, I have painstakingly worked out, is to peel and fold. Peel and quickly fold. Peel the corner and then fold the peeled corner under, so that it sticks to itself and not to my arm or my leg or my head. Yes, this is much better than unpeeling it all in one go.

"Come on. Come on. Come on," I mutter to myself as I hear Mrs Elliot's voice outside the door asking Year 5 class to *quieten down*.

"Nearly there. Nearly there. Nearly there," I hear Bella muttering on her side of the bag.

Throwing the label 'Bicarbonate of Soda' onto the floor, I turn quickly to look at Bella. The door to Year 5 classroom has been opened. As the door opens, there is a rush of wind like the sound of a gust blowing across the playground. Following behind, the quiet air in the room is filled with tapping feet and mumbling voices.

Before I've even had a chance to take a big gulp to prepare myself, before I've had a chance to go over the next part of our plan in my head, or ask Bella if she's ready, the bag is closed. Immediately, in complete and utter darkness, the whole bag violently swings to the left and I am thrown as it moves. Flying through the air to the side of the bag, my shoulder hits the closed zip, before I bounce off it and fall to the floor with a very painful bump.

"OWWWWWWWWWWWWW," I cry, sitting on the floor in the dark, not sure whether to rub my shoulder or my back. "That hurt soooooooo much," I whisper through the pain.

"Here is your bag, Mrs Elliot."

I know that voice. I know that voice! It's a voice that jumps my heart into my throat. It's the familiar fake sickly-sweet voice of Charlotte. Charlotte has Mrs Elliot's big black bag. No wait, Spinosaurus-Charlotte has hold of the bag that we are sitting in!

With another swing to my right and then to my left again, I cover my head with my arms. A spatula flies past my head followed by a plastic petri dish. All the crunched-up labels roll towards me and then away from me as I try to grab hold of something that isn't moving. I have no idea where Bella is. I can't see her, I can't hear her and the swinging bag is making me feel so sick that I don't want to move my head.

Is it the swinging bag or the fact that Charlotte is holding it?

What if she opens it?

What if she drops it?

"Oh! Be careful there, dear," I can hear Mrs Elliot calling out.

"I am," Spinosaurus replies.

I think I'm definitely going to be sick – I cannot take the swinging motion any longer.

"You must be very careful with my bag," Mrs Elliot says, now sounding much closer. "Here, let me take that from you. Right, everyone, sit down and silence, please!"

With Mrs Elliot carrying the bag, the big rocking motion has stopped. I still feel sick but at least I can lift my head up. Looking up, there is a line of light coming in from the top of the bag and this helps my eyes get used to the dark. The floor is a complete mess. The glass tubes are luckily all still in their holders – phew! Everything else is a mess. The rolls of labels, petri dishes and spatulas are all mixed up and everywhere, and there, on the other side of the bag from me, is Bella.

"Are you alright?" I ask, as I crawl slowly over the mess and head towards where she is sitting.

Bella has both her hands on the top of her head and her face is all tightly screwed up. "Yeah, fine, my head just hurts a bit."

Clearing a space to sit down next to Bella, I can feel my body completely and utterly shaking. I'm shaking from being thrown around the bag, the fact that Spinosaurus-Charlotte was so scarily close to the bag and close to finding us, *and* from the fact that Mrs Elliot now has the bag. She is so near to us and that means she is near to our plan… Our plan!

"Bella, I haven't finished the top line!" I nudge my head up and towards the top row of glass tubes on my side, the light from the top of the bag showing a neat row of labels still on the glass tubes.

"Quickly," Bella urges as I jump up. "Before she opens the bag."

With my shaky hand on top of a tube of clear liquid, I pull myself up, one foot now on the tube, the other on a tube of white powder next to it. My hand reaches up to the next row. There is still a slight rocking of the bag as I climb, and this just makes me feel even more wobbly. There's no time to try and steady my feet; I lift myself up to the next row and find a place for my hands and then a place for my feet.

As I get up to the top row, the rocking of the bag now feels like the swaying of a boat on the sea. I grip my feet firmly on the lids of the row underneath and I get to work with my technique – peel and fold. I then grab hold of the second purple holder, move myself over so that I'm standing in front of 'Epsom Salts', and then once more I peel and fold.

Throwing that label down to the floor, I'm ready to move on to the next glass tube when the bag comes to a complete heavy stop. I'm holding on to a tube of 'Citric Acid', my feet are balancing on the tube below and I freeze. My heart is thumping so hard in my chest that I feel like it is about to burst, except I cannot move at all.

"Today we are going to look at crystals," Mrs Elliot says.

"She's showing them something on the whiteboard," I whisper, as I imagine myself sitting in the classroom in my seat, at the table, watching her. She will have her black bag on the table in front of her, the whiteboard set up with today's lesson and she will be standing there with the whiteboard pen in her hand, smiling at us all. "I've got time," I whisper to myself, hoping that my body will unfreeze itself. With my hands shaking again, I fumble to peel off the 'Copper Sulphate' label.

The next two labels are a lot easier now that the bag isn't moving at all, even if my hands are shaking. I'm nearly there. With my foot ready to move to the next glass tube and my hand already in place, I start to move over. In that moment, a bright light flashes before my eyes, making everything suddenly very clear before being too painful to look at. I close my eyes, nearly completely lose my balance, and end up standing with both feet on one lid with my arms now hugging a glass tube full of blue powder. I blink over and over again. There is a large shadow slowly appearing from the left of me, like a solar eclipse of the sun with a trail of coffee-smelling air. I want to scream. I know it's got to be Mrs Elliot but it's still a really big head and it's still scary. Quickly, I squeeze my whole body as much as I can into the row of tubes. In-between two glass tubes, I stand there hoping that it *is* Mrs Elliot who has opened the bag and ultimately hoping that our plan has finally worked.

"Well, for all my days I did not expect this!" the coffee-smelling voice booms.

The chatter of the class goes silent and instinctively I hold my breath.

"Of all the things," Mrs Elliot continues, her face disappearing and the light now filling the bag again.

With the giant head now gone, I lean out of my hiding place and look down at Bella. She is crouched down at the bottom of the bag, a litter of scrunched-up labels all around her. She is looking up at me while holding tightly on to one of the spatulas, her eyes big and wide.

"I would never have expected this!" Mrs Elliot yells, and I hide again.

This is it. Here and now, there is about to be a whole heap of big enormous gigantic super-gargantuan TROUBLE and with my Spider-man-like trouble sense going absolutely crazy in my ears, I think my head might explode!

Chapter Fourteen

Trapped

"Of all the things!" Mrs Elliot shouts again, her voice sounding further away.

"What is it, Miss?" someone questions.

"Yeah, what is it?" another voice asks.

My heart is thumping, I can hardly breathe, and my hands are completely sweaty and definitely still shaking. I look down at Bella again. Bella does not look well. Her face looks clouded and distant, as if someone has just told her the worst news in the whole entire world. Then again, listening to Mrs Elliot, maybe Bella has been told the worst news in the whole entire world – Mrs Elliot is not happy. Bella loves our extra science lessons with Mrs Elliot, and perhaps with this, Mrs Elliot is her favourite teacher and all she wanted was to save her from Tammy and Charlotte and their evil plan to ruin her science lesson and get her fired.

This is stupid; I should be sitting down there with Bella and we should face this punishment side by side, not with me hiding like this. Climbing back down the tubes again, my legs are trembling as my feet find a lid to stand on. I walk through, crawl and fall over the mess on the bottom of the bag so I can reach Bella and give her a hug.

"Thanks," Bella says through a very thin smile.

Before I can say anything about it being OK, or that I'm sure Mrs Elliot will forgive us, or something that might try and cheer her up, a new shadow appears across the bag. Like a cage falling down upon us, I look up to see a hand with sprawled fingers diving into the bag.

I guess this is it, I think completely to myself, not wanting Bella to feel any worse than she already does. The whole class will see us now and we will be in deep, deep, deep, deep trouble. TROUBLE.

Ready and waiting, I watch as the hand enters

and comes straight for me, the huge fingers close to my head, and I wonder if the class will laugh at me. I wonder what Mrs Elliot will say and if she will use me as a warning to all children everywhere not to open a teacher's bag. I wonder if she will leave me like this, all tiny like a mouse, and I will have to spend the rest of my life this size and I will die old and grey as a constant reminder to everyone who ever meets me that this is what will happen to you if you let your friend open a teacher's bag.

And then I wonder what Mum and Dad will say when they see that I have been shrunk and I am now a much smaller version of my previous self. Will I still be allowed to sleep in my bedroom? I've always moaned that it's much smaller than Darren's room but now it would be huge for me. Will they let me keep it or will I be moved to a box or a metal cage like Harry-the-Hamster?

What will they do?

I feel an ache deep down in my stomach – a heavy, weighty, achy feeling. Perhaps I will be in so much trouble that I will never be allowed to watch TV or do anything in peace *ever again*.

As I'm wondering all these things and planning my life with no TV and only a little box with a plastic wheel as a bedroom, I realise that the hand isn't actually reaching for me at all. It isn't reaching for Bella either. The fingers go straight past us and grab the tube above my head, smoothly unclipping it from its purple holder. The tube is taken out of the bag. I see it being carried away by the giant hand with its giant gold ring and I imagine the tube as one of us. I can hardly breathe as I watch it. The shadow disappears and I try to breathe and then blink and then swallow but my throat is completely dry.

"Now silly, silly, silly me," Mrs Elliot begins, her voice light and cheerful. "Look, everyone, I seem to have forgotten to label my chemicals today, which is not like me at all! Isn't this perfect, though – we will have a lesson on identifying chemicals."

"But, but I thought you were going to show us an experiment today," Charlotte's familiar voice booms.

"That is true—"

"Yes, you said you were going to show us an experiment," Tammy jumps in.

"But I have no labels on my chemicals!"

"No labels?" Tammy questions. "But they were labelled earlier—"

"Sorry, what was that, Tammy?"

"Nothing," she mumbles. "I just mean, like, you usually have labels on them, don't you?"

"Yes, I do, and I wonder why I don't have them today… Yes, William, you have a question?"

"Can't you still show us the experiment?" he asks.

"It could be very dangerous if I were to get my chemicals all mixed up. You see, look, this tube has a clear liquid inside it. Now, it could be just plain old tap water, or it could be, say, sulfuric acid."

The shadow appears. The giant hand reaches in quickly and then, as if by magic, takes two tubes swiftly from their holders.

"You see, these two tubes have clear liquids in them too."

The class sighs in one big Year 5 breath, all ready for a really long afternoon of talking and writing and with no fizzing or bubbling or snake-like tongues leaping out.

"OK, OK," Mrs Elliot starts to say, and the class goes quiet again. "I'll tell you what, if you can help me to identify the right chemicals, then I will show you some really cool experiments."

"Yesssssssssssssssssss!" Year 5 class all hiss together, and with this I can feel my arms relaxing.

The constant sick feeling in my stomach is still there, but I can breathe and I can blink again. I really thought she was going to grab me and show me to the whole class. I can't believe she didn't. She must have seen us. She must have known that we were the ones that made all this mess. I'm so confused. Mainly, though, what I really want to know is:

"What happens now?" I say to Bella. When we thought up this plan to warn Mrs Elliot, we didn't really get to the part of her actually finding us or us actually succeeding in warning her and what happens afterwards. "What is the next part of our plan?"

Bella opens her mouth to answer, or perhaps to say she has no idea either, when another voice distracts her. I can hear it too. Through the cheers and sounds of a now-happy Year 5 class, I can hear Charlotte's voice trying to get Mrs Elliot's attention.

"Mrs Elliot," she says again, her loud voice unmistakably booming out. "I notice that Bella isn't here."

"And Clara," Tammy adds.

"Oh yes, that is true! And Clara too… I wonder where they could be? They were definitely in school this morning."

"Yes, I definitely saw them this morning and at lunch," Tammy confirms.

"Would you like me to go and tell Mr Graveshead that they are missing? I really don't mind."

I watch Bella, her face now burning red. "Oh no," she whispers. "What are they doing?"

I shake my head slowly, unsure what to whisper back. I try to work out what we can do about this horrible situation of us not sitting in our seats and us actually sitting in the bottom of a big black bag. I can't believe Charlotte and Tammy. I can't believe they are still trying to get us into trouble and Mrs Elliot fired! Great! We finally have a plan that worked and Charlotte and Tammy have *another* back-up plan.

Do those two ever run out of good plans?

So now, Bella and I either get into serious

trouble for missing school OR we get into serious trouble for opening Mrs Elliot's bag and shrinking to the size of Harry-the-Hamster and then Mrs Elliot gets fired too. I cannot believe they are going to win after everything we have been through. I can feel my trouble Spider-man-like sense starting up again.

"Thank you, Charlotte, there is no need to worry," Mrs Elliot replies, sounding very close to the bag. "Or you, Tammy."

"But they should be here and they are not."

"I know."

"She knows?" I whisper to Bella. Well, of course she knows, she must have seen us. She must have seen us and instantly known what had happened. I guess, deep down, a small part of me just wondered if maybe she hadn't actually seen us in all the mess at the bottom of her bag.

"Bella and Clara are accounted for," Mrs Elliot says. "And that is all you need to know on the matter. However, seeing as you are *so* keen to help me today, you can start by telling me: what are the basic physical identifiers we would use to recognise a chemical?"

Wait. Does this mean our plan worked?

Our plan has actually worked.

Our plan has actually most definitely worked!

We have completely managed to warn Mrs Elliot and stop her from using the chemicals in her bag. We have stopped Tammy and Charlotte in their evil plan to '*shake the class up*'. We have stopped them and their crazy reign of good luck. AND we have saved our science lesson. Our plan *actually* worked. I really did not think it was going to work.

Although, technically, we are still the size of a mouse and we are sitting in Mrs Elliot's big black bag awaiting our punishment.

"We did it," I say to Bella, as I hear Mrs Elliot mention the periodic table, her voice moving around the classroom. "We warned her."

"Thank you for your help," Bella replies, which really makes me smile.

*

"We are doing some serious chemistry detective sleuthing here," Mrs Elliot announces as Chloe follows her instructions to stir a small amount of white powder in water.

It may have been like having a whole slightly muffled lesson with my eyes closed, but so far the class have identified chemicals using:

Colour.

Smell.

Magnets.

And they used a special strip of paper to see if one of the clear liquid glass tubes had an acidic chemical in it.

It sounded like a good lesson, as usual, and Bella looks completely gutted to be missing it – she has not said anything in absolutely ages and her bottom lip is sticking out further than I have ever seen it stick out, ever, and her eyes look completely miserable.

"Tammy and Charlotte should be sitting in here, shouldn't they?" I whisper, nudging Bella, as we hear the class making 'OooOooo' noises.

Bella tries for a smile, which looks more like someone has drawn a thin line on her face in red pen. "Can you imagine if *they* had been shrunk?"

"Well, I think it would have been really hard to stop myself from squishing them with my big giant shoe." I laugh.

"No, I mean – imagine how much trouble Mrs Elliot would be in if she had actually shrunk *them* instead of *us*."

"Oh, I guess I never thought about that... Yeah, they would have screamed and shouted and ran around telling everyone. No, wait, I know, they would have run immediately to Mr Graveshead so they could twist the story around to 'Crazy-Elliot' being a dangerous teacher! They would have got exactly what they wanted – Mrs Elliot fired and our extra science lessons cancelled for good."

"Yes," Bella replies with a nod, her grumpy face returning.

"So, really, you opening her bag and shrinking *us* instead of *them*, well, that also saved our science lessons," I conclude, smiling at Bella. "You did it. We did it."

Lifting her head up, Bella smiles a genuine smile this time. "Yeah, we did, and you know what? Only two weeks till our next Mrs Elliot science lesson."

Chapter Fifteen

On the Move

Mrs Elliot's big black bag is moving. The whole bag is moving and rocking, and Bella and I are still sitting inside it, both of us holding on to the sides as we sway to the gentle swinging motion.

It didn't start gentle. It actually started with the whole bag suddenly lifting high up in the air, my stomach leaping up and then falling back down like on a rollercoaster. There was no warning. Mrs Elliot was still talking. The lesson had hardly even finished – none of the usual handover to Mr Graveshead or starting the class on free reading. Before Bella and I knew what was happening, the bag leapt up into the air and swung out of the room.

"Where are we going?" Bella whispers, holding on to the side of the bag with both hands as the balls of sticky rolled-up labels jump around with us.

"I think we are going down the stairs," I reply, the bag jumping up and down before being thrown to the side as it makes a sudden right turn.

With her hand firmly gripping on to one of the purple holders on the bottom row of test tubes, Bella looks up at the opening of the bag. "Can you hear anything?" she says quietly.

I try and listen out for any familiar noises. "No, nothing," I reply, batting away a ball of sticky label that is trying to attach itself to my head.

Bella and I had been tidying up the bag. While Mrs Elliot had carried on with the lesson, quickly grabbing chemicals out of the bag and closing it again, Bella and I had tried to tidy the mess on the floor of the bag. It was my idea. Sometimes, when Mum and Dad are on the edge of being in a really bad mood with Darren or me, or if I've done something that I really totally did not mean to do – like leave my lunch box at school before the start of the summer holidays

– I tidy up my room. It seems to cheer them up if my room is tidy. If I tidy the bathroom up a bit too then this definitely gets them out of any bad mood.

So, in an attempt to stop Mrs Elliot being really angry with us, we tidied up the bottom of the bag. Neat piles of clear petri dishes at one end, the metal spatulas all together along one side and the plastic box with glass rectangles at the other end, with the rolled-up labels in a pile in the middle.

A complete waste of time.

Another sharp corner, and the spatulas fly across the bag as Bella and I cover our heads. The pile of petri dishes falls over and spreads across the floor and the labels are everywhere. A left turn, a few more paces, a sudden stop and the bag is a complete mess again.

"We've stopped," I whisper.

Bella nods and as she does so, there is a definite noise of a door opening – a quick metal clicking sound and a slow creak. The bag moves a little bit further before a quick drop, a stop and then it is filled with bright light.

"You two had better come out," Mrs Elliot says.

Bella looks at me, a horrified look on her face,

which I have rarely seen from her, but I can only imagine it is the face that I pull every time Mr Graveshead says there is going to be a surprise test. I give her my best genuine reassuring smile, and since her hands are still firmly holding on to the purple holder in front of her and she does *not* look like she is going to move, I start to climb up and out of the bag first.

Up the rows of test tubes like a skilled mountain climber, I find a place for my feet before reaching up for a place for my hand. Then, at the very top and next to the shiny metal Malteser-like clasp, I look out at the view.

The bag is on a table and in front of me is a giant Mrs Elliot. She is sitting on a chair at the table, her hands clasped together, her forehead crinkled into an angry, disappointed frown, and she is staring straight at me. She is humongous and she looks angry. I can't look at her.

Looking around, anywhere else but at Mrs Elliot's frowning face watching me, I realise we are in 'The Staff Room'. The big black bag is sitting in the centre of the round table in the centre of the room. As I climb down the leather strap on the bag,

I notice that 'The Staff Room' has not changed since my very first glimpse of it when Mr Whitehead stood holding the door open. There is still the same pile of cardboard boxes in the corner of the room, a mountain of teacups on the draining board next to the sink and there are still pieces of paper everywhere. As I climb off the leather strap onto the table, I look around the room and then quickly back at Mrs Elliot before looking away again. It's OK, she's now watching Bella, who has appeared at the top of the bag and has started to climb down.

I don't know what to do or where to stand, so I step slightly in front of the bag, and not too far from it. It feels like I'm standing here, in the quiet room, very still and not moving, for absolutely ages. Eventually, though, Bella jumps down from the handle and comes over to stand next to me.

Mrs Elliot breathes in a really long breath. "Well," she finally says, the tips of her fingers connecting as if she is making a den with her hands.

"Mrs Elliot, it was all my fault!" Bella blurts out, the words exploding from her like a firework.

"No, no, it wasn't," I manage to say while she takes a deep breath of air.

"Yes, it was!" she immediately retorts, her eyes fixed firmly on Mrs Elliot's large frowning forehead. "I was the one who heard Tammy and Charlotte say they were going to do something to the chemicals in your bag to '*shake the class up*' and I was the one who said we needed to guard your bag, and I was the one who got all worried because I thought they had already done something to your bag, and I was the one who opened your bag to see inside it."

She stops abruptly. Mrs Elliot and I are still staring at her, and while I want to protest at what she has confessed, it is kind of all true. I close my mouth and turn back to look at Mrs Elliot, who I can see is still processing Bella's extra-long sentence.

"Really, well," Mrs Elliot says slowly, but just as she's about to take a breath or say anything to us, I too realise that I cannot take any more of this.

"And I was the mouse Mrs Cullings saw!" I shout really loudly, my own confession exploding like a fresh round of fireworks. "I was the one who scared her!"

They are both looking at me, both looking stunned by my outburst. Bella looks extra confused, which is when I remember that I have, up until now, failed to tell her about the mouse mistaken identity incident with Mrs Cullings, or tell her that Mrs Cullings may or may not have tried to tread on me. I am still opting for the idea that she wasn't trying to tread on me at all but that she was in fact just jumping all around me in a scared fear-of-mice type way with very big feet.

"And I'm sorry," I add quietly at the end, because I am.

"I see," Mrs Elliot finally says, her head still nodding even though she has stopped talking and everyone in the room is quiet. "Well, this is all very serious."

Bella looks at her feet and the table underneath them, and I decide to look down at my feet too. It seems like a good way to stand as we await our punishment.

"I should put you both in detention, tell Mr Graveshead what you did and tell your parents – you snuck into a classroom during lunch break and opened a teacher's bag. This is all very serious…"

I can see Bella out of the corner of my eye; she remains completely unmoving with her eyes still watching her feet and so I remain still too, standing right next to her as we listen to Mrs Elliot. This is our punishment and this is the BIG DEEP TROUBLE that we have got ourselves into.

Yet, as I stand listening to Mrs Elliot, I can't hear my trouble Spider-man-like sense. There are no crazy, scary feelings going on in my head and I realise that I don't feel that deep-down dread that I thought I would be feeling. I don't feel lost or upset or wishing that I could turn back time and make sure that none of this ever happened. Perhaps, here and now, it is OK being in trouble. I don't need to be afraid of what Mrs Elliot is saying, or what Mr Graveshead is going to say, or what Mum and Dad will say, because I can handle it. I can handle detention; I can handle Mr Graveshead shouting at me and getting really angry. I can even handle Mum and Dad finding out and then me having to eat dinner for the next however many weeks with them talking endlessly about how I shouldn't have done the thing that I did at the point at which I did it. And I can even handle being sent to my room and not being allowed to watch TV. I can handle all of this because Bella and I were on a mission. We were on a mission to do something about something instead of just letting the world go by. We were standing up for something that we believed in and something that we knew was wrong. And if it means being in trouble, well, I don't mind that, I can handle it. Here and now my Rule Number One: Avoid Trouble, can be broken.

"But," Mrs Elliot says, another big sigh pausing her sentence, "I guess I can overlook it all and I can say you missed class because you were doing a special job for me."

"Really?" Bella says, looking up at Mrs Elliot, her face suddenly alight at her favourite teacher.

"I guess you *were* doing a special job for me, after all."

"Really?!"

"Yes… and I should never have put that silly trap on my bag. I suppose, in hindsight, it could be considered… unfitting."

I'm confused at her choice of words, but I smile back at her anyway. "That's OK, Mrs Elliot," I say. "At least we still have you for our extra science lessons."

"Thank you, Clara," she replies with a nod and a big crinkled smile. "Oh, and as for your size," she adds, dragging her big black bag around us and over to where she is sitting, before placing it on the floor next to her. "Unless you would like to stay this size..."

"Oh no, please no, no, no, not at all," both Bella and I mumble.

"...Then, you'll both need two drops of this," she finishes, bringing out a bright pink label-less liquid and a pipette. "Only two drops, mind you, we wouldn't want you to grow too much!"

Too much? How much is too much? I instantly think, keeping this thought to myself.

Chapter Sixteen

Taller Than Reggie

In the days that pass since our shrunken adventure, my favourite red bench in our school playground just doesn't feel the same. I sit on it. I slump down and pull my coat sleeves over my hands. I fall down into my coat so that only my eyes are appearing out from under my hood. But it doesn't feel the same. I can't sit still. I just can't sit.

And other things feel different too. For example, I can't look at Mrs Cullings anymore or look at her navy-blue shoes. When she comes anywhere near me at all, I instantly want to run to the nearest wall where it is safe. Bella says this is completely natural after all we've been through and it should pass with time.

I have also stopped letting Tammy and Charlotte push me around like they did before. Like when they used to say silly little comments to me or sit next to me and copy my work. They have stopped this and have also stopped pushing in front of me in the lunch queue. Standing in the queue, my eyes fixed on the sausages, peas and mash potato, with chocolate chip cookie and ice-cream for pudding, they paused next to me. Nothing and absolutely no-one was going to get in my way of my pudding today.

"No," I said sharply, looking into Tammy's eyes. I still can't look at her shoes without feeling dizzy.

Without saying anything, she moved further down the queue behind us. It was the tastiest school lunch ever and I ate it really slowly.

They seem to know that I won't let them push me around anymore and we have reached a kind of unsaid understanding. I am hoping this one does not pass with time because I like this. If anything, there is a confused look bubbling across their faces every time they look at Bella and me. They whisper.

They stop. They keep their distance. They watch us and then pretend they weren't. I think I might keep my eye on them two, just in case.

Other things, well, I tried the rope ladder in Ms Morgan's PE class yesterday and I am sure I got much further than I did before. She didn't say anything to me but I know I did.

Bella and I also sat with Mrs Elliot one lunchtime and went through every glass tube in her big black bag – which doesn't seem as big now, but I am still scared of it and I didn't really want to touch it or sit too close to it. We tested every one of the chemicals, with Mrs Elliot's help, and we re-labelled them all. In conclusion to our experiments: nothing was mixed in with any of the chemicals and there were no new chemicals that weren't already there before.

"They must have swapped all the labels around and maybe where the tubes were in my bag," Mrs Elliot concluded, placing the tubes back alphabetically.

*

"She has definitely made you taller!" Reggie shouts again for the third time, as he sits in-between Bella and me on the red bench in our school playground, under the open window to the school kitchen.

"You are just imagining it," I reply, trying not to grin, which is really just hurting my stomach because I need to laugh.

"Clara, I was taller than you, I should know. She's added like 5cm and it's not fair!"

"Are you sure you were taller?" Bella asks, as all three of us watch a stray football bounce past us, with Ben running just a few paces behind it.

"You know I was," he mumbles, as the three of us turn back from watching the stray football to watching Year 4 taking their turn on the climbing frame. I sink my head into my coat once more, my hands twisting and closing off the sleeves, shutting off any gaps for the cold air to get me. "And..." Reggie says, slumping further into the bench, "just to top off my really bad day, Mr Knight said they are cancelling lunchtime athletics club – I mean, it's just—"

"What?!" I yell, sitting upright, my head bursting out of my coat.

Reggie jumps in his seat, looks at me and then blinks several times. "Something to do with a timetable clash, I think he said."

“This is outrageous!” I protest, my hands now bursting out of my sleeves so that I can slam my right fist down on my other open palm.

“Well, I… I didn’t… it is?” Reggie begins to say, his eyes open wide as they stare at me.

“You know what?” I continue, undeterred, standing up and stepping away from my favourite red bench. “We need to do something about this!”

Bella lifts her head out of her coat and smiles at me. “Yes! I’m in.”

Matador